THE HAUNTING OF GRANDMA CROWLEY

TROY MCCOMBS

Copyright 2020 by Troy McCombs

Licensing notes

Chapter One

The dead don't always stay dead...
not when they have a link to bridge the gap to life...

Danny Willow was fourteen when his grandma, Ethel Crowley, died of old age. At fourteen, the prospect of death seemed like an illusion, a rip in the construction of reality. His mind couldn't grasp the concept well; but then again, whose could at any age? Who knew where we went, if we went anywhere, when we died? There were plenty of religious zealots who thought they had the answer, but no one *really* knew because nobody returned after their heart stopped beating and their veins stopped pumping blood.

Grandma Crowley's death impacted Danny almost immediately, at the viewing, when he began to see and hear strange, strange things.

His mom got the call late Saturday night, 3:00 a.m. or so, from his Uncle Lanny, Ethel's caregiver and son. He'd been taking care of her for years—lifetimes in dog years, Danny assumed. Her ailing health had been in steady decline for most of that time, almost as long as he could remember.

His mom was evidently worried when she looked at the caller ID. "It's my brother," she mumbled to dad. Danny had shuffled to his door to watch her. The ringing phone had torn him out of a light, restless sleep. He aimed an ear and listened.

She had the phone to her ear for only seconds before she wailed, "No! Oh no! No-ho-ho-ho."

Bad news. Someone's died.

David, his dad, woke up and embraced her as she fell back down into bed. She cried quietly, somberly, in the most bleak and depressing way. Danny didn't realize then that this may have been when it all started, when this got the ball rolling, but he'd be wrong. This just felt like the beginning of something inherently bad, malevolence brought to life.

Then his mom shut off the phone and told his father, "My mom... she's... she's dead."

"Oh God. Oh, I'm so sorry, honey." He still sounded half-sleep, and only half as glum as she did.

Could've been exhaustion, could've been, but David and Ethel had never gotten along. He'd always harbored an inexplicable aversion to her which no one—David included, he would've told you—understood, even though they hadn't spoken in months. She'd always shunned him for being the strong, outspoken, self-righteous man she made him out to be. He had a tendency, which was actually more of a bad habit, really, of sparking heated debates with anyone who questioned his personal beliefs, whether political, religious, or whatever.

His parents embraced, mom crying, dad doing his best to soothe her. They were lit by yellow-white slashes of moonlight shimmering in through the spaces between the Venetian blinds hanging from one of the windows of their room. They hugged for some time, and Danny stood there watching, lingering, not moving, feeling... *weird.*

Even though nothing happened that night, nothing unusual, anyway, that was the first night Danny felt unnerved. Because Grandma Crowley had passed on? Because his mom was upset and weeping? He didn't know.

***

The viewing was just a few days later.

Dressed in the darkest ensemble he owned: a black, suede button-up and black Dockers, along with black socks and black Perry Ellis dress shoes, he and his parents left for Lancing's Funeral Home. The drive took ten minutes. They lived in

Ducougery, a half-rural, half-suburban town of about two thousand citizens. Lancing was one town and four traffic lights away. Of course they hit every red light, and when Danny glanced up at one of them, he thought of what it meant in terms of life and death. *Red. Stop. Go no further. Move no more. Never speak again.* Then it turned green—*Go. Live. Laugh. Breathe*—and the idea faded away.

His dad parked on Pike Street, behind a black Chevy Cobalt and in front of a banana-yellow mustang. People walked east along 5th, toward Lancing's Funeral Home. Not a lot, but some. Danny knew a lot of them, but not all. A few looked old enough to be in the midst of death, themselves. There was a hunched-over geezer hobbling along with the help of a derby cane, a blue-haired woman pushing a walker at a snail's pace, and a woman recklessly navigating a motorized wheelchair. Danny felt dismayed by the first thought he had: *these people, too, are going to die soon.* Time had done a number on them, reducing them to bones, wrinkles, liver spots. All apparent life seemed to have gone away, leaving them with fragile, nearly-useless vessels. *I never want to get old. I never want to move that way. I don't want to look like a zombie. They look terrible.*

"Earth to Danny?"

Danny blinked his eyes and looked at his dad. He had unbuckled and turned to him in the driver's seat. "You okay? Looked a little lost there. Daydreaming?"

Danny shook his head. *Sure, Dad, just daydreaming about how awful it's gonna be for me in seventy years.*

They all got out of the car, a maroon Honda Accord. It was new, still smelled that way, fresh off the assembly line. Dad was making payments on it with his recent bonus from Harlow Linn, of Harlow Plastics, a factory that made plastic containers. The Honda sure outclassed the unreliable 1999 Ford Taurus junk-mobile he'd had for the last decade or so. Now it was a lemon in scrapyard heaven.

The fall air was chilly and carried with it the stench of dead leaves, which covered the brick-paved streets in a plethora of fiery colors. Danny contributed the smell to Halloween, one of his favorite holidays. He still had no idea what he wanted to be this season, and only had a couple of weeks yet to decide. His routine would be the same, though: eat too much candy, scare people, and watch horror movies.

Nasty wind blew through several maples. Their limbs shook more leaves to the ground. Soon, it looked like it was snowing autumn colors. The smell intensified, and Danny took in a big whiff.

He smiled and stepped up onto the curb. The smile waned when he came back to the present and remembered where he was, why he was here. Poor Grandma Crowley. She'd passed on to some great beyond, and they were going to see her for one last time before they buried her.

His palms started sweating and his heart began racing when they walked into the building. There were a lot of unfamiliar old-timers inside, all dressed in black clothes, some crying, others telling stories, some drinking, some eating. A new smell overpowered the one of dying leaves: dying people. Danny attributed this smell to hospitals and hospices, worn-out bodies and pungent perfumes. The stench of the old that followed them as closely as the Reaper did through what remained of their short, mundane lives.

Danny couldn't really understand why, but he wanted out of here. Some unbidden impulse advised him to leave, go home and think about old age and death much, much later. He fought through the panic—even though he saw the door in hindsight—and stayed put. He stayed because that's what his mom and dad would've wanted, because that's what Grandma Crowley would've wanted, too. He ignored his deepest instincts to pay his respects.

Music was playing. The kind of analogue stuff from the thirties or forties. The instruments sounded inorganic and out of tune. A woman sang in an airy voice about the end of the world. It only added to the eerie atmosphere of the funeral home.

His parents greeted people, some he knew, others he didn't. He had no interest in talking. Curiosity carried him forward, farther into the building, closer toward the bouquets of flowers and the coffin up ahead. It felt like an otherworldly power was pulling him toward the first dead body he'd ever seen. He could not curb or control his inquisitiveness; the almost sentient determination in his legs propelled him through the crowd, past more repulsive smells, between too many strange people, and closer to Grandma Crowley. His initial panic was fully replaced by a need, a confounded urgency to glance upon the deceased. He hadn't seen Grandma for months, when she'd emerged from the top room in her house out on Ray Lane, and wondered if she looked the same. She'd looked halfway dead then, her face a road-map of wrinkles, her skin sagging and swaying, her eyes vacant and dull, her arms and legs defying her. She could barely use the walker then. Just closing her mouth had been a feat for her; it instead remained open in a mummified expression that'd make anyone with a glint of life uncomfortable. How bad did she look now?

How bad, indeed?

Danny pushed and *excuse-me*'d his way through what felt like a hundred people. At last, he managed to step out of the growing throng of mourners and into some breathable space.

There she was, Ethel Crowley, lying like a statue on white linen in a box, hands on abdomen, the hundreds of wrinkles on her waxy face covered with make-up. She wasn't smiling, wasn't moving, wasn't thinking, wasn't feeling, was simply gone. A body without life. Was this the end of the road for her? Had she ceased to exist? Blinked out like a candle in the wind? Or was some part of her still alive elsewhere, in some far-off region of reality that living people couldn't glimpse? Either way, it was an overwhelming thing to consider at any age, much less fourteen. Death. The ultimate red light. The point of no return.

He couldn't look away. Her frail corpse lay there, unresponsive, and he stood there, flooded with emotion. But they weren't the feelings a boy should've had for his deceased grandmother. They didn't include positive memories or pleasant experiences. A bubbling cauldron of animosity surged through him, a simmering brew he couldn't control or understand. The unbidden resentment turned his heart black, poisoned his internal light, everything that made him feel good. He forgot about his parents, about the guests, about the funeral home, about everything. He was caught in a morbid spell, like a fly trapped in a spider's web. Then the fear hit home. He wasn't sure if his eyes were fooling him, if he was daydreaming, or if he was hallucinating. It didn't look real, that was for sure. Grandma Crowley's face started to move. It seemed like it took hours for her lips to pull in opposite directions, forming a malign smile by some diabolical internal force. The movement was almost unnoticeable at first, happening so slowly that one could attribute it to overactive imagination. It frightened Danny so badly, he felt every hair on his body stand up. His veins turned cold and shrank. His mind refused to believe it, but his body told him it was real. And she continued to smile. Her old skin continued stretching until her make-up cracked, until her tissuey flesh ripped and decayed teeth poked through, flashing a sinister grin. Danny then heard her, speaking to him alone, using some means of telepathy. "Dannyboy, your grammy loves you. She's dead but not gone, and is coming back for you!" Her voice sounded darker and hoarser and grittier than he remembered, like a chronic smoker's with chopped metal packed in her throat. Far from human and parsecs from decent, it rattled the ground beneath his feet.

Her face was spreading, breaking, splitting, ripping. Void of blood, the underlying tissue looked white instead of pink. Roaches and centipedes made their presence known seconds later, crawling with avid life that Grandma Crowley didn't, or shouldn't, have had. One long worm pushed its way out of one eye socket; roaches swelled in her nose and came scurrying out both nostrils. Maggots swam in her black, bottomless mouth. Danny couldn't tell where the bugs ended and the teeth began, it was all so terrifying, and he just stood there, unable to move, breathe, or call for help. He was stuck in a living nightmare alone with his dead grandmother who was somehow, someway evil.

He thought he heard music just then, the loathsome and discordant notes of an untuned violin, followed by the vocals of what could only be evil. It rose, rose, the harsh noise increasing in volume and intensity.

The bugs were in multitude now; they covered Grandma Crowley completely. All he could see beneath were a few wisps of her colorless hair. But still, he could sense her smile, her undying malice for him, and could no nothing. She'd trapped him where he was able to get away easily, savoring his fear, apparently, and he knew this wasn't the end of her. Life went on when you died, he realized, and not all afterlives were amiable places filled with sunny souls.

The music climbed. The bugs sprouted wings. The inherent smile grew. Dizziness upset Danny's balance, and he started to sway. A heavy weight fell on his shoulder, squeezed like a vice, and when he blinked his eyes again, he snapped out of it. Grandma Crowley lay in her coffin, undisturbed by bugs, her face no longer torn but her wretched grin quite noticeable.

"You all right?" his father asked. His hand was resting on Danny's shoulder. The music faded into something less ominous.

The horror exploded. Danny turned and ran, through the gathering of mourners, almost knocking one old man to the ground in his flight, and outside, where he could breathe and gather himself.

What did I just see?

No people occupied the streets, and no vehicles droned past. A heavy breeze ripped leaves from trees and blew them furiously.

Why did I just see that?

Danny's legs shook beneath him. His arms tingled. His heart pistoned in his chest, the rampaging thump drumming steadily in his ears.

I haven't seen the last of Grandma.

"Dannyboy," he recalled her saying, "your grammy loves you. She's dead but not gone, and is coming back for you!"

No, this was the beginning of something bad.

Chapter Two

The Willows headed home only minutes after that. His parents knew something wasn't right; his dad frequented looks at him in the rear-view mirror, and his mother repeatedly asked him what was the matter. He lied and said he had a stomach ache, even though he knew she wasn't buying it.

What I saw wasn't real. I imagined it. Maybe it was a hallucination.

Uh-oh, what if it's a brain tumor that caused me to see that?

He didn't know what was worse, the thought of having cancer or being affronted by his dead grandmother. The implication almost made him laugh.

On the way home, they didn't hit any red lights. That scared him worse. *Green. Return to life.*

By the time they made it to Tinney Lane, rain began to fall. It started as a lazy drizzle, errant drops here and there, before progressing into a steady, angular shower backed by thunder and lighting.

Dad pulled the vehicle into the garage. Wipers flung water off the windshield and onto the shelves and yard tools hanging on the walls. The garage door closed in its slow, methodical way, making Danny feel trapped.

Dad turned the key, killing the motor. He got out. Mom turned in her seat and looked at him in the back. Her face was a black outline. Her somewhat frizzy hair brought back images of his grandma. "Honey, are you sure you're okay? What happened in there?"

"Nothing."

"You seemed fine until you viewed the body. Did it upset you, seeing her like that?"

All Danny could think about was seeing her unlike they had, covered with bugs from the inside out. Her repulsive voice had twisted the core of his guts. In his mind's eye, he saw her moldy, wrinkly hand snatching onto his and holding him there until he was dead, too.

Grammy loves you, Dannyboy. Always and forever!

He shook the thought and looked away, ignoring his mother's questions.

Danny ate a box of pizza rolls, a peanut-buttered sandwich, and some pop tarts, trying to quench his hunger. It hurt to eat with such a queasy stomach, but it had been nagging him since, as if the brief encounter had rendered him physically weak.

Mom suggested they play a board game, but Danny told the truth by saying he didn't feel well. Dad asked him if he wanted to watch a movie. Danny said *Not today* and went upstairs to his room, feeling his parents watching him as he entered and shut the door.

He laid in bed, laced his hands behind his head, and felt an incongruous mixture of dread and comfort. It felt good being home in his familiar bed, but the sense that it was all going to turn sour, rendered comfort almost aloof. He gazed upward, not focusing on the ceiling, his mind elsewhere and nowhere at the same time. Rain pelted the window, sounding more like hail rather than water. Flashes of lightning brightened his walls, his Metallica posters, and thunder bellowed angrily, like the grumbles of a large dinosaur stomach.

He didn't remember falling asleep.

The slumber he fell into was not interrupted by bad dreams, but the uneasiness that lingered never went away.

Thunder woke him sometime later, five loud bangs, until he realized they were knocks on the front door.

The rasps brought him back into a strange reality he wanted no part of. The sinking spot in his gut felt like depression.

He heard his mom and dad greet somebody. Then he heard that somebody's voice: Uncle Lanny's.

He was a short, pudgy, bald man who moved and spoke

ostentatiously. His mouth never quit, not with food or with words. His head was mellon-like, ugly, the hair that used to occupy it now abundant on his limbs. He wore glasses that magnified his fiery, piercing yellow-green eyes. When he looked at you, they trapped you. You'd know this without returning his gaze. He hadn't had a real job since his mid-twenties, before Grandma Crowley had taken ill, and that was just a gig at a grocery store some eleven years ago. Danny didn't like him. The hairy ogre was too loud, too annoying, too much.

"Daaaanny!" his mom called. "Uncle Lanny's here!"

Danny cursed into his pillow. Company was the last thing he wanted right now, and Lanny was the last person he wanted to deal with.

Except Grandma...

He took his time in getting up, cursed some more, sighed for good measure. Rain trickled against the glass to his right. Looking out, he saw that the curbs were swollen with water, and Tinney Lane looked like a gloomy wasteland.

Danny joined everybody in the downstairs lounge area, a small, square room equipped with a sixty-inch television, suede brown sofa, floor lamp, Danny's beanbag chair, and a recliner. Plush, white carpet, backed with padding, blanketed what had once been a concrete floor. Mold-and-mildew-resistant drywall covered cinder blocks and ugly, overhanging rafters. A series of ten steps connected this room to an upper first-floor hall at one end. There were also two small windows mounted into the foundation. It was a cozy, comfortable spot where Danny spent a lot of his time—sometimes more than his own bedroom.

Mom, Dad, and Lanny were sitting together on the couch; Danny sat in his beanbag chair. Lanny watched him enter with those eerie eyes of his. *Please don't stare at me.*

But Danny's attempt at telepathic communication was unsuccessful. Lanny stared and unwittingly hypnotized him, his mellon-like head reflecting scarce light. Sometimes Danny felt this way in his uncle's presence, literally unable to turn away from him when he glared, as if Lanny had a hold on him, trying to capture his soul by sight alone.

"How you doing, Dan?" Lanny had only started calling him Dan recently, cutting his name short for reasons Danny didn't wish to know and didn't care to ask.

"I'm okay," he mumbled.

Lanny tilted his head slightly. The corner of his mouth twitched into something that resembled a creepy little smirk. Then again, a lot of what Lanny did came across as creepy. He walked with a strange limp and had an unusual, hunched posture... but that persistent gaze of his—that was the worst of all. Danny had never been around him before without being overwhelmed by the aroma of Old Spice. It all simply made you wonder.

Danny had a friend who'd met him once. After shaking his hand, Randy cringed and suggested that he and Danny go outside. In the yard, Randy had told Danny that Lanny *Creeped him out.*

Lanny smiled—smiled normally, and Danny dismissed the thought.

"You'll be okay," Lanny said. "Grandma Crowley really loved you, Dan. You were her favorite. She always said you were special. You are. She's looking down on you now, watching down on you from heaven."

Danny didn't feel any heart strings being tugged; he instead felt someone sprinkling black mar on them. Lanny's words were giving Danny the creeps.

Lanny reached out and took his hand with sweaty, rough, calloused fingers. Danny almost drew away—actually started to, as a matter of fact—but saw his parents both smiling at him from the corner of his eye, and accepted Uncle Lanny's wet, hard hand. Felt like a pliable, wet stone.

His uncle started weeping, and his mom wrapped her arms around him and rocked him like a baby. Danny's discomfort level increased slowly but steadily, and all remaining daylight was swiftly fading. The room would have been pitch-black had the television not been on. Of course, it was on RLNO7 News. His parents ate it up. They always had to keep up on things. When you were a kid, though, those events mean nothing. You watched TV for fun, not for gloom.

Lanny's pathetic sobs made the room and atmosphere seem so much darker and melodramatic. Danny couldn't help but feel a negative presence hovering around them. Didn't have to be a ghost; it could have simply been the bitter bereavement of Grandma Crowley.

Danny wanted to believe he'd imagined the vision at the funeral home. He wanted to disregard the idea that Ethel was coming back from beyond the barrier of death; that she was still the kind old woman who used to buy him Blizzards and clothes, a saint without so much as a sprinkle of spite.

But he just couldn't.

And Lanny's being here, his exaggerated reactions, only added to it.

Nobody said anything for some time, except for RLNO7's Don Hubart and his report on yet another missing child in Lancing. That made a total of eighty-two disappearances within the past twelve years. The authorities hadn't found so much as a clue, either.

"I don't know what I'm going to do," Lanny said, withdrawing from mom's cocoon. "I've been taking care of her for so long. That's all I knew. She's all I had."

"That's not true. You have us. You've always had us."

He wiped his tears away with the back of his hand. "I didn't mean it like that. I just mean... I lived with her everyday. Everything I did—I did it for her. Because of everything she did for me... for all of us. I miss her. Part of me's died with her."

Part of her is alive with me, Danny thought nervously. *Some part of her hasn't let go, and...*

He brushed the thought away so forcefully, he actually shook his head.

"You okay?" Dad asked him, inquiring with furrowed brows.

"Yeah, just... nothin'."

"Looked like you were clearing bugs out of your hair or something." Dad laughed. Dad laughed, and it actually lightened the mood, put a little levity back in this bleak time of mourning. But when Danny looked back at Lanny, he noticed those cold, predatory eyes peering into his. Lanny was sitting at an angle where neither his mom nor his dad could see him. Any trace of sadness appeared to be gone. His lips were pinched firmly together, and his face was a blank canvas.

Danny's heart galloped.

Then Lanny smiled at him, and Danny felt a fast rush of relief. Uncle held nephew's hand, and this time, Danny accepted it a little easier and more quickly.

"She's in a much better place, Danny, and she isn't suffering any longer."

Danny nodded. *That's the first time he used my full name in awhile.*

"That's right," Mom said. "She can walk without her walker..."

"She can fly with the angels." Lanny smiled.

Dad said, "She doesn't have to worry about her dentures flappin' when she talks, 'cause they're real where she is now."

Everybody laughed. Mom had begun to cry—something Danny had managed to miss until now. Dad was glued to the TV, his eyes fierce as can be. He aimed a large remote at the Insignia and upped the volume, quieting the gentle laughter and heightening the gloom again, this time audibly.

"Jesus," he said. Pixelated light brightened his face in a plethora of colors. "Twelve years and not a clue. Not a body turned up. No leads, no nothing. Either aliens are abducting these kids, they're all running away, or there's some real sicko who knows how to do it and not be caught."

Lanny took interest, turning his head to the prime light in the room. Mom did, too.

"They should find that monster," Lanny added, "if it is a child abductor, and execute the sucker. Save everyone the trouble. Don't have a hearing, don't waste the taxpayers money; just get him and fry him. Bring out old sparky like they did in the old days."

Photos of several kids appeared on screen, dissolving from one to another in sequence. They all looked happy, healthy, precious. There was a boy dressed in a gaudy plaid sweater who was laughing hysterically; a girl with pigtails grinning away despite her missing front teeth; a toddler in pajamas moving letter blocks across a carpet.

Mom shook her head. "Who could do that? How could anybody be so evil as to abduct such innocent children and do God-knows-what to them? I can't even..."

"What they should do is hang 'em upside down by his groin," Dad said, "and torture the bastard. That's what he deserves."

"Nothing worse in the world than someone who hurts children," Lanny said, nodding assertively, his bald head reflecting light.

All Danny could think was: *If there is someone out there, doing bad things to kids my age, younger than me, will it ever be over? Will they ever find him?*

Lanny left some forty minutes later, after mom fixed a small mountain of spaghetti for everyone. The four of them sat around the kitchen table, which regularly went unused except for during the holidays. Any other time it supported laundry, books, magazines, newspapers, junk mail. Danny and his dad liked to eat downstairs. Mom loved eating on the back porch in the spring, summer and fall, then in the living room during the winter months. Tonight they ate and shared stories of times past, of experiences they'd had with Grandma Crowley. Nobody picked up a phone. Nobody left the table to check on anything. Everyone did what they'd done in the old days: enjoy each other's company. It was as simple as that, and that simple.

For about twenty minutes, Danny felt okay. Good, in fact. Marvelous. Lanny invited him to stay the night sometime, now that he didn't have Ethel to take care of, to which Danny accepted. It was a white lie, of course. Uncle Lanny and Grandma Crowley's house smelled *weird,* and no prize or reward in the great wide world interested him enough to get near that house again, at least not for quite some time. And Danny did get time that particular evening: eating with those he loved, his family. That tainted feeling he'd had since the funeral home had almost subsided completely. In a child's developing mind, a good experience can offset one of fear—that's what dinner had done. But later that night, when the moon rose and darkness settled over the town of Ducougery, Danny found himself in a predicament most people never find themselves in. Not even in several lifetimes.

He was in bed at ten. His shades were drawn, the moon peeking through tiny slits. Until now, he'd forgotten about the incident—*or hallucination*—at Lancing's Funeral Home. That's all it could've been. A trick of the mind. He'd heard about Occam's Razor in school. All things considered, the simplest explanation is usually the right one. That was the logical way to approach it.

He blinked his eyes. His heart began to settle, slow, and his mind calmed wonderfully.

Danny closed his eyes and breathed in long, deep breaths.

"Danny...."

The voice was so faint and ethereal and far away, he thought it was just the wind.

I didn't hear nothing. I'm going to sleep now.

The storm had moved toward Herrington, but the wind was still mighty, blowing leaves against the window.

Just the wind, that's all. Grandma Crowley's dead and gone...

"Danny..."

The voice was closer. Unmistakable this time. Definitely not the wind. He kept his eyes shut and strove to ignore it. The kind, comforting pleasure of exhaustion broke apart in wisps. A loud, shrill squeak at the corner of the room startled him. His eyes shot open. But it was just the tree branches scraping against the window, their skeletal-like limbs moving almost deliberately.

Danny closed his eyes, squinting them shut. *Go away...*

"Danny boy!"

He jumped in bed. The voice was very close, and clearly one he'd heard before. Grandma Crowley's. She'd come back to claim him.

But why?

His heart galloped its way into hysteria, beating with the ferociousness of a rampaging animal. His mind sought to find answers to questions he didn't know how to ask. He gripped the edges of his covers with hands that looked like claws.

"Mom?" he called. Maybe it was just her. *Yeah, my mom yelled for me, and I just mistook the voice for...*

"Oh, Dannyboy! Your grandma's here!"

Her voice sounded impossibly black, remarkably demented, and ever closer. He could actually feel it more than he could hear it.

His eyes flitted to the door, which began to creak open. The nightlight from the bathroom was his lone source of illumination of the hallway beyond.

"Grandma...?" Danny cried, tears pricking his eyes.

The door creaked. The hall became more visible. The bathroom light faded, as if evil were swallowing its burning coil.

"That's right," he heard her say in that horrible tone. "I'm coming soon, Dannyboy, real soon, just for you. I eat from the fruits of innocence. We'll be able to do things that can defy time, space, gravity, reason. We'll inflict pain upon your parents, upon you, upon anyone we choose. Does that sound like fun? Oh, it will be. It will be! And do you know the irony of all this? This is your choice, Danny. Through you, I shall grow and progress like a weed. A dark, malignant one that eats life and light with great efficiency. I'll never grow old again, you know that? I'll never grow old, and death will never clamp its pathetic hands on this soul ever again. And you thought I was an ill old hag for the past several years? But I will show you, oh, God, I will show you the power I possess! Yes, Danny, we shall attain the strength of high-level demons, the ability to fly and levitate and control fate. It's so nice where I am. You'd belong. The darkness! The great and complete, everlasting darkness! Where worms never stop eating and pain only stretches and expands. Where light cannot exist. Where death only eats. You belong. *We belong... to the black goat of a thousand young!* He is your father now, and I am your new mother. Fourteen days, my child. Fourteen more days to the end, and then you will see the most distasteful sight you ever saw!"

The light flickered, faded some more, and Danny had just about enough. The voice, the tone of it, the creaking door, scared him into a frenzy. His heart felt like it was about to rupture. The bathroom light was on the verge of going out, and if it did, and he found himself blind in the darkness, he would just flip out—

The light didn't go out, not then, anyway. It stopped its fitful game and stayed on, seemingly even a little brighter than he remembered it being. It was a slight comfort, but just not enough, so Danny turned on his bedside lamp. He stayed up for some time, sitting on the edge of his bed, mulling over what happened, why it was happening, and what exactly would happen in fourteen days.

I believe that's Halloween.

Chapter Three

Danny didn't remember falling asleep, much less lying down. His dad woke him sometime around seven, after having stepped on him while getting out of bed. Danny, it appeared, had brought a sleeping bag into his parents' room and crashed on the floor.

"What are you doing in here?" his dad asked. "Why aren't you in your own bed?" He looked drunk when he was tired and zombified right after he woke up.

Danny looked up at him. "I dunno. I just wasn't feeling good last night."

"Well, how are you feeling now?"

"I'm okay now," Danny said, lying through his teeth. His chest felt hard, burdened with stress and fear and dismay. Last night felt very recent.

Telling his father what he'd seen and heard the night before would've helped, he believed, but he couldn't do that. Not yet. Not here. Not at this moment in time. He was tired, his dad was exhausted, it was too early, and not enough had happened yet.

He tried telling himself that it had all been a bad dream, but in his heart, his blackened young heart, he knew that that was a fairy tale.

I'm afraid this fairy tale doesn't have a happy ending.

His dad stumbled out of the room.

Danny soon got ready for school. He brushed his teeth, ate cereal, packed his book bag, and left. He felt a small sense of relief after leaving, as if the hanging cloud of despair had broken, even if by just a little bit. The day was cold and crisp, the sidewalk covered with more dead leaves that his dad would probably make him rake up later. Clouds blanketed the sky.

Danny walked up Charles Street, crunching over thousands of dead leaves, headed to the intersection of Wilham and Barnivue where the bus would pick him up. He wasn't sure if he was willing to tell Randy, his best friend, about his encounter with his deceased grandmother, on account of being ridiculed. Danny doubted Randy would, but he didn't want to take that chance. Besides, this was bothering him. He still hadn't ruled out the possibility of a mental disorder. He was fourteen, and didn't schizophrenia usually begin during young adulthood? Randy had told him stories, big and small, about his cousin Lidia, who had schizophrenia. The tales were scary. She saw things and heard things and felt things and believed all sorts of nonsensical stuff that could never be true. So Danny decided to rule out the obvious before he attributed this to the supernatural.

The streets remained empty as he made his way to the bus stop. Diana Reed and Gretchen Popolv, two neighbors of his, weren't here today. Diana was a pretty, pudgy girl with braces and a grating laugh that could annoy a monk. Gretchen was an uptight cheerleader who tramped anyone she considered below her. How the two of them were friends, beat Danny.

He was glad he didn't have to listen to a hyena's guffaw or a goody-two shoe pretend he didn't exist.

Maybe they were sick. Maybe they'd gotten a ride. Danny didn't care.

A chill breeze threw leaves into the street, where they danced around in a tight, almost uniform cyclone over a manhole cover. Danny pictured the Tasmanian devil whirling his way along Wilham Street, and cringed at the sudden, inexplicable coldness that struck him. Felt like ice slipping through him. A moment later, the foul taste of death filled his mouth. He took a few steps back, stepping away from both elements.

A voice came out of the breeze, which died suddenly. Sounded like, *Daaaaaaanny!*

He shook his head and waited on the bus. All the houses looked dead, unoccupied. Maybe, he wondered, he'd stepped out of the real world and into the Twilight Zone. *Those shows are fiction. They're not real. Ghosts are figments of your imagination, you know that. What's going on is you're developing a mental illness. Schizophrenia. Think about it. You watched those bugs crawl and fly out of grandma's mouth. One second later they were gone. And dad had been standing right there when it happened. You need to see a head doctor, not a witch doctor.*

The bus pulled up a moment or two later. He got in and rode down Wilham.

Mrs. Briner's first-period science class was full today. Mrs. Briner herself was tardy, and while the class waited for her, eighth-grade teenagers gabbed.

"Sorry to hear about your grandma," Randy consoled. "I lost my grandma last summer. Not this past one but the one before."

"How'd she die?"

"Stroke. She came out of it okay, but days later she slipped away. Complications or something. How did yours?"

"Old age, I guess. She was old. I mean old."

"How old was the old broad?" Javier Hiller asked. He sat adjacent to Danny, in a seat with *Mother's Milk* and *I love Ass* scratched into the desk. The boy was missing one of his central incisors, due to a fight on the playground years ago. He had far-set fish eyes and hyper-activity coming out of him like steam from a train. Danny didn't have hopes for the kid. He got into trouble more often than Randy did, and Randy was trouble with a capital T.

"You want another tooth knocked out of that mouth?" Randy asked Javier, the only kid in the room dumb enough to mouth off to someone two years older and three times as big.

Javier turned around in his seat.

Joking, Randy asked Danny, "While we're on the subject, how old was she?"

Danny smiled and tore his eyes away from the chalkboard. "103, so my mom tells me."

"Damn. That is old. I don't think I wanna live that long." Life for Randy wasn't a great one, either. He often came to class with bruises and cuts on his face, and always played them off as being *accidents* or *sports injuries* whenever anyone asked about them. Danny figured that everybody was wise to it by now, though. Not even James Grim, the lamebrain in the front row, was that dim. Randy described his own father, whom Danny had never met, as a *beer-guzzling hot-head with a fuse shorter than a millimeter that has its own ignition source.*

The boys had been friends since seventh grade, barely a year ago, when Randy got into a scuffle with Tony Salong, a bully with bad acne and a worse temper. Randy had instigated the fight in the lunch room because of some derogatory remark Tony had made. Randy knocked the bigger kid on his butt before the principal came in and broke it up. Everybody in the room pointed to Randy with accusatory fingers, but it was Danny who Principal Redding looked to. And it was Danny who lied and told him that Tony had thrown the first blow.

Danny didn't know Randy back then, but he knew and loathed Tony.

Since then, the two had become almost inseparable.

Mrs. Briner, the shortest and widest woman on God's green creation, entered the room minutes later. When she walked up the center aisle, Danny felt his desk wobble. Everyone quieted as she took the front of the room, her face saggy and wrinkled, like worn, droopy leather. "Okay, class," she said, "take out your textbooks. Turn to chapter three. We're going to go over something called photosynthesis."

Danny took his Earth And Science book out from under the rack beneath his seat. Others did the same. Randy sighed and flipped off the teacher while she wasn't looking. Danny stifled a laugh.

Mrs. Briner wrote something on the board. She was wearing a muumuu, one of about ten she owned. Nobody in Ducougary High had ever seen her in slacks or a blouse, and she'd been wearing the same tennis shoes since about the dawn of man.

Letters appeared, words formed, sentences took shape. Danny listened to the pleasant sound of chalk against board, almost hypnotized by it.

"Can anyone tell me what they think photosynthesis is?"

Hands went up. Neither Danny's nor Randy's was one of them. Danny scribbled inside his notebook randomly, sleepy, uninterested.

"Jonathan," the teacher pointed to Jonathan Ridley, the kid in the front row. He was small but fiery and wicked smart for his age. "Photosynthesis is process by which plants eat—they absorb and convert sunlight and rain into their own energy source."

"Correct," Mrs. Briner said enthusiastically. "Whereas we eat and process food for energy, that's what plants and algae do with sunlight. It uses it as fuel. Now, there are two types of photosynthesis: oxygenic and anoxygenic. While they are similar, oxygenic is most common. During oxygenic photosynthesis, energy from sunlight transfers electrons from water into carbon dioxide. This produces carbohydrates. Water becomes oxidized and loses electrons. Oxygen, or H_2o, is produced along with the carbohydrates. Photosynthesis takes in carbon dioxide and that's produced by organisms that breathe, and reintroduces oxygen. Without photosynthesis, there'd be no air, and we couldn't breathe. We'd suffocate from all the carbon dioxide. So, we're dependent on them."

Danny continued to scribble, slowly coming aware of today's science lesson. He yawned, sleepy, wanting to nap. Why did he have to know about how plants lived? About how they supplied oxygen to mankind? He wasn't going to be a botanist.

According to Grandma Crowley, or his wild hallucination, he only had fourteen days left.

Fourteen days and counting.

Math and history were even more uneventful and unendurable than science. At 11:30, Danny and Randy went to phys-ed class. It was located on the southeast wing, and served as a lunchroom as well. There were basketball hoops set up at opposite ends of the room, racks brimming with balls of all sorts, tables folded up into walls, overhead lights that cast the most repulsive shades of yellow. Mr. Milik, the teacher, had extraordinary muscles, a face that was always red, and a voice like a drill sergeant. Danny didn't hate the guy, but he didn't like him much, either. Mr. Milik stood somewhere in that particular *Eh* section where Danny couldn't care less about him unless he was bleeding from a neck wound.

"What are we doing today?" somebody asked. Danny couldn't see who it was through the throng of kids, and couldn't place a face to the voice. The room was already hot. Some of the teenagers were sweating, and Bobby Gradison's body odor was as suffocating as the carbon dioxide Mrs. Briner had been talking about. Randy coughed.

"Well," Mr. Milik said, "how about a nice game of dodge ball?"

They started the game after they did their routine warm-up. At least half the kids were already huffing by then, but Danny wasn't one of them. He stood in the back where the teacher couldn't see him well, and did his banal exercises lackadaisically. He started to sweat by the time Mr. Milik carried a massive blue bag of balls out of a closet. A boy laughed as someone made the joke, "You got a lot of balls, Teach."

Others laughed, too.

"Dannyboy..."

Danny turned his head toward the voice—the open doorway—and felt time stop.

There she was, standing at the end of a long corridor, bathed in darkness, her frizzy white hair sticking up in coils, motionless. He couldn't make out one feature other than her hair, which began moving. Things came out of it, protrusions of some sort, and it took Danny a moment to realize they were horns. They grew slowly, crunching through skull, down-turned instead of up, spilling blood, tearing through flesh. Though he couldn't see her face, he could feel her sadistic smile.

She just stood there.

Danny just stared.

Out of his peripheral vision, he noticed Randy looking in the same direction.

"Do you see it?" He had no idea why he referred to her as an it, but that word seemed more appropriate.

Randy looked back at him, brows furrowed. "See what?"

Pain impacted Danny's face, smashing his nose and throwing a dull ache throughout his entire body. Tears flowed from his eyes, blood from his nostrils. A groan escaped him. He covered his face the second the dodge ball bounced off it and the scent of copper took precedence over Bobby's body odor. Kids surrounded him. Mr. Milik ran to him. But the only thing concerning Danny was that smile, those horns, that cadaverous gaze.

And the fact that Randy had seen absolutely nothing at all.

Silence filled the room for some time. Mr. Milik had Danny tilt his head back to stop the bleeding, but all that did was upset his stomach. All the blood just went downward. The ball had also managed to cut his lips. But at least the pain was short-lived. "It broken?" Danny said nasally. The teacher made him sit in a chair. Everyone else in the room stood around like witnesses at a car accident.

Mr. Milik grabbed his beak and moved it from side to side. "Does that hurt?"

"Not really." Danny doubted whether the man knew what he was doing; he was a gym teacher, of course, not a doctor. The dumbfounded expression on his beet-red face declared he had no idea. The gawking, to him, was worse than anything else.

"I'll send you to the nurse," Mr. Milik said.

"You sure you're okay, man?" Randy asked him.

Danny gave a thumb's up. But he would've been a lot more okay, dandy, even, if Randy had witnessed what he had at the end of that darkened hall.

The school nurse, Amy Gilligan, ended up examining Danny. She looked a lot more certain when she inspected his nose, nodding, her eyes big and welcoming, her face a little pallid and a lot softer. She had him tilt his head forward and said, "Makes you sick, doesn't it?"

He nodded from his elevated place on an examination table. The room was the epitome of clean, and also nearly stark white. Overhead fluorescent bulbs bathed the small room in bright, even light. The smell of disinfectant was strong but not overpowering. Through a series of windows behind him, rain lashed the world outside.

"It's definitely not broken," Nurse Gilligan told him. "But they can bleed like faucets if hit right. In fact, I've seen broken ones that didn't bleed as much as yours has."

"Really? Wow." News to him. He kicked his legs nervously about.

She took notice of this and creased her brows in a look of concern. "Nervous?"

Do I tell her I'm losing my mind? That I'm seeing things that aren't there? Hearing stuff that upset my stomach a lot more than this blood?

Her obvious concern grew as she watched him.

That's when Danny stopped moving his legs. "No, nothing."

Her worried brows creased as far as they'd go. She looked at him more endearingly than his own mother had in years, he thought, as he turned his head to the rank of windows and surveyed the nasty storm.

"Well, if you ever need to talk, I'm here, Danny."

Almost involuntarily, he blurted out, "What's the typical age when schizophrenia can start?"

And yet her brows creased even further, making her look unattractive and stupid. "What do you mean? Do you think you have schizophrenia, Danny? Have you seen things? Heard things that others didn't?"

He nodded. Blood ran out of his nose once more, circumnavigating around the red-drenched tissue he was holding up to it.

"What have you seen? Heard?" The lines around her eyes evened out. Her face was perfectly smooth again.

"Just... stuff."

"What kind of stuff? You've gotta tell me, sweetie, 'cause if you are, this is a serious matter. And, yes, you are in the age range of the onset of this disorder. It's a very nasty disability. I know from experience."

"Seriously?"

"Yeah. It actually runs in my in-laws family. Without the right medications, it can be life-changing, debilitating."

Rain assaulted the windows behind him. "What happened to them? What are all the symptoms?"

She wheeled closer to him on her stool. "Well, I'm no psychiatrist, but there are different symptoms, and it manifests differently in different people. Visual and auditory hallucinations are a common one, feeling imaginary bugs crawling on you, agoraphobia, irrational fears, extreme paranoia, delusions, believing things that have no basis in reality. Have you experienced any of these things? Please let me know if you have, okay, Danny? Like I said, this is a serious matter that needs to be taken care of."

A sense of relief came over him just then, and the rain slacked.

"It's okay, really," she said, "just go slow and tell me, okay?"

He nodded and looked into her eyes. "Okay, here's what happened—"

He barely made it off the tarmac when something stopped him cold in his tracks. It not only prevented him from spilling his guts; the twinge of fear struck him with more potency than the kickball had. Two things happened in that little white room. First, the overhead lights flickered. That could have been caused by the storm, yes, or perhaps faulty wiring, definitely. But that wasn't what frightened Danny. What did was the frizzy mass of white hair and repulsive face peeking over Nurse Gilligan's shoulder—Grandma Crowley, her face blackened by mold, maw open and crawling with centipedes.

The horrible vision scared the piss out of Danny—quite literally. The odor was immediate and acidic; the warmth pervaded his lap and stained the paper on the examination table under his butt. He didn't think he screamed, he really didn't, even though after witnessing such a revolting sight, screaming seemed like an absolute necessity. He was vaguely aware of falling backward, sliding, and plummeting to what felt like a fifty-foot drop to a sticky, recently-mopped floor. Nurse Gilligan's face disappeared, because only Ethel's visage held his rapt attention. And Danny knew what the manifestation meant—he knew that immediately. The dead woman was sending a message, one that harked, *Do not dear tell another soul about me.* He got the message loud and clear. He understood it on some primitive level where the fear had an alias, an identity, and a depiction. In fact, it scared him so badly, he even lost consciousness. Reality died, and only naked, unadulterated terror reigned.

He didn't become lucid until his mom came, picked him up, and drove him home. A good half-hour of his life had simply melted away. He didn't remember Nurse Gilligan helping him up off the floor. He didn't remember her phoning his mom with the speed of a first-responder. He didn't remember walking to his mom's car with his arm wrapped around the nurse's shoulder, and he didn't remember his mom talking to him while he sat next to her in the passenger-seat.

His grandma's loathsome face was seared into his mind, his very psyche, forever like a rotten splinter of unrelenting meat.

Chapter Four

His mom's voice finally came in when they rounded Pierson Avenue, just miles from home. She was crying, sniffling, her hands shaking on the wheel. Danny felt like a zombie beside her, staring out the window, his wits not quite back. The world looked bleak and blurry, encumbered by chronic rain.

"Are you okay?" she asked.

Haven't I heard that question from a bunch of other people today?

He nodded. He was afraid that, if he told her the truth, Ethel's horrible face would appear in the rear-view mirror. He didn't want to scc it, so he shrugged and watched the rain.

"The nurse was extremely concerned about you. I'm extremely concerned about you, honey. What happened in there? She said you screamed—so loud her ears rang—and tumbled off the table. Then your eyes were rolling, that you weren't quite 'there.' Like you'd had some type of bad panic attack. And, she said, before you fell, you were asking about the symptoms of paranoid schizophrenia? Why, sweetie? What's going on? I'm worried, I mean, really worried."

Danny avoided every mirror. He zipped his lips as well.

What do I do then? Just what the hell do I do?

Thirteen days...

Gotta do something.

"I can't tell you right now, Mom. I wish I could, but I can't."

"Why? Why can't you? Are you really seeing things that aren't there? Tell me, Danny, I'm your mom. I need to know. If it's something bad, we can fix it. I'll help you. Dad'll help you. I have to know. I'd give my life for you, sweetie."

"I know." He managed a smile. And she'd managed to pull one of his heart strings.

At least I have reinforcements...

Which don't mean crap when you're dealing with the supernatural.

He had things to brood over. Neither Randy nor Nurse Gilligan had seen Ethel, and he had, so that meant one of two things: either her death had somehow inadvertently triggered his visions... or she was legitimately back to haunt him. Danny longed to cling to the former. He'd simply take some medications, see a therapist, and live with it. He'd put all this behind him and lead some kind of normal life. Best case scenario. Worst case scenario: Ethel was after him. But why? After all the candy and toys over the years, after hundreds of hugs and thousands of kisses, why would such a sweet old lady without a bad bone in her body want to harm him? And her grandson, of all people?

None of it added up. Nothing made any sense.

Then, another possibility floated into his adolescent brain: *Unless she made herself known only to me...*

If only I can see her.

He mulled over all this while his mother drove.

They were home before he broke free from his tormenting thoughts. The garage door closed with a long, slow hmm, shutting out drab daylight and muffling the deluge.

Mom shook him. "Danny!"

"Huh?"

"We're home now."

They went inside. Mom's trembling was worsening, and Danny felt bad knowing he was causing it.

He turned on every light, opened every blind to make sure the place was lit properly. He did this discreetly, away from his mom, because he didn't want to worry her any more, but he figured she'd catch on eventually.

Danny just wanted to feel safe—excess lighting seemed like the prescription.

The house looked somehow dreary and different. It didn't feel like home anymore, either, but rather a waiting area. One where you sit and wait anxiously for Death to come strutting in with his sickle in one hand and your number in the other, his voice dark and deep as he declares to everyone: *your days are about to end!*

"Why did you turn all the lights on, Danny?" Mom said, sneaking up behind him in the hall.

He turned, with a little start.

"Really, Danny, tell me, otherwise I'm gonna drive myself crazy."

He took in a breath. Closed his eyes. Braced for whatever followed.

"Yes, I'm seeing stuff. I don't know what they are, but... I'm scared, Mom."

"What are you seeing? Are you seeing anything right now? Other than me standing here?"

He kept his eyes closed.

"Danny, please look at me."

He opened them, expecting to see the worst, but saw only her standing there, the hall around them and the kitchen behind her. Nothing abnormal at all.

Of course I didn't tell her what I saw...

"It's just us... for now," he told her.

"What is it that you've seen, or saw?"

He avoided her eyes, pretending to ignore the question, maybe let it fade. But she looked serious. He couldn't lie. He couldn't get out of this stare-down for anything.

"Scary things. Evil things. Monsters that have been taking the shape of..."

"Of what? Grandma?" She smiled, almost laughed in reflex. Instead of embarrassing him, it relieved him.

No lights flickered. Grandma Crowley didn't appear from out of nowhere. Nothing happened. In the moment, it felt wholly uneventful. Danny let out a deep breath.

"You say you've been seeing evil visions of Ethel? When? When did this start? What did she look like? Where? How?"

He explained, and let nothing go unsaid. He felt quite uneasy as he described everything from the bugs up to the incident in the nurse's office. Mom nodded, listened carefully, without judgment, the whole time holding his hand. As he talked, the rain slacked and the sun came out. He didn't know if this was some kind of sign or omen, but he was feeling better, getting all this bottled-up tension out into the open.

When he was done, his mother smiled endearingly. "Yes, that's schizophrenia, honey. You just need help. You know your grandma would never, ever hurt you. Don't you?"

He shrugged. She held him. "I love you. Grandma Crowley, up in heaven, loves you. She would have given you the world. There's no way that what you saw was a ghost or a monster. I've learned about this in college."

"You have?"

"Yes. I minored in psychology. I've even had the chance to meet people with schizophrenia, first hand, and lemme tell you, it's some scary stuff, believe me."

He smiled. "I don't have to believe it. I am it."

She smiled and gave him another hug.

She didn't wait to get him help. She didn't go through the tedious process of scheduling an appointment, filling out papers, or any of the other banal tasks involving seeking treatment. She didn't even turn off the lights; they got back into the SUV and drove to Mannor Run, a psychiatric hospital for adolescents. During the forty-minute drive, she called Dad and informed him. Danny didn't see any unholy sights in that time, and knew, in his heart of hearts, that this was all going to be over with soon.

Chapter Five

The road leading to Mannor Run was a disaster, replete with craters, cracked asphalt, broken chunks of black rubble. Mom took the sinuous curves, which meandered the property, slowly and carefully. Fields were overgrown with weeds and goldenrod. Tires climbed over the broken road like bulldozers over wrecked debris. Danny watched the sun sparkle over a motionless pond. Vehicles parked in the lot reflected errant rays, looking almost like laser beams.

Mom parked in a handicapped space beside the entrance. "I don't care if I get a ticket. All I care about is seeing you well, okay?"

He smiled. "Okay."

Inside, the woman at the front desk asked how she could help in a brusque voice. She was a dark-complected woman whose real skin tone was impossible to determine. Danny didn't know whether she was black, white, or had had a terrible experience at the tanning salon. Her fingernails were long, fake, and rainbow-colored.

But Mom was more brusque. "I'd called about twenty minutes ago, about my son."

"Danny Willow?" The woman checked her chart.

"Yes!" Mom's tone amused Danny. "He needs to see a psychiatrist, now, today."

"Um, Mam, he either has to be admitted or make an appointment—"

"No, no, no! He's frightened me half to death, is himself scared half to death, and needs to talk to somebody, now."

The woman raised her voice, "Mam, don't yell at me. If you want him to see someone, you either should have called ahead of time, or you'll have to admit him."

"No!" Mom was yelling. "I did call ahead of time, lady—"

"Earlier ahead, Mam." She was nearly yelling, too. "Then he'll have to be admitted."

Mom smacked the desk, hard. Smiling, Danny looked around to see how much attention she was attracting.

The waiting room was pretty bare; only three of the ugly blue contour chairs were taken. The other twelve were empty, and one was covered in crayon doodles. Coloring books cluttered the two small tables. An older man was reading a newspaper and avoiding the drama at all costs, so it seemed. The other two seats were occupied by a middle-aged couple. The woman in green was weeping quietly, her boyfriend-husband consoling her.

"He is not being admitted!" Mom shouted. Danny turned back around to her and Miss black-or-white. "If you don't page a doctor to see my son, you—"

"Do you want me to call security? The police?" Miss black-or-white was shrinking back, but Mom, he could tell, was just getting started.

"Good, call the cops. Go ahead, get security. I don't care."

"If you want him to see a doctor, Mam, he must be admitted. That's policy, the law. There's nothing I can do, because I could lose my job. Okay?"

Mom pointed at her, trying desperately to say what obviously wouldn't come out. She looked devastated.

"I can't officially evaluate him, but I can chat with him for a few minutes." This voice came from the entrance.

It was male, and sounded smooth and patient.

Mother and son turned at the same time. Standing there against harsh sunshine was a tall, lean man who looked as old as Lanny Crowley. He was wearing a pink polo t-shirt, tan khakis, a glistening watch, and cool sunglasses. He looked and sounded like a human chill pill.

Miss black-or-white said, "No, you don't have to—"

"I want to."

They spoke in a corner of the room, Danny and Dr. Mindling,

alone, away from everyone else. In the meantime, Mom went outside.

"Ever since she died, I've been seeing her. Her face is falling apart, caving in. Bugs crawling out of her eyes and mouth. She says things that make no sense—and her voice—her voice is so dark that it hurts my stomach. It's like a living, waking nightmare. In fourteen days, she told me I'm going to die."

Dr. Mindling's eyes were big and calculated. He took this information in as if he heard it all the time. He evinced little worry, always looked poised. Danny trusted him and felt very comfortable around him already. The sharp sting of his cologne was strong on the olfactory sense.

"Well, I'll be honest with you," Mindling said. "It is not really your dead grandmother. If I were to make an educated guess on what you're experiencing, I'd say you were traumatized when you saw her in the coffin. You said you'd never been to a funeral before the other day? Never saw another dead body?"

"That's right."

Mindling nodded assertively. "I think it's trauma, and it may have led to these manifestations. However, that does not rule out the possibility of schizophrenia. The schizophrenia may have been triggered by this event, although I can't say for sure."

"So, what do we—what do I do?"

"First off, we'll need to evaluate you, do some tests of your brain, just to see what's going on in you, and to see if it's physiological. Then we'll have a better idea. And if it is schizophrenia, you may have to take medicine for it."

"How long will all this take?"

Mindling smiled gingerly. "By the end of today, young man. I'll put everything through on my end, okay? Now, I can't offer any guarantees, and it might take a couple of days, but I know how stressed you must be."

"Am I gonna have to be admitted?"

"No. Let me see what I can do. I'll be back in awhile. Just sit right here. I shouldn't be long."

The man got up and walked to a big set of double-doors, which opened with a key-card he removed from his pocket. He entered. The doors, attached to two elbow hinges, swung shut quickly with a brush of warm air.

Dr. Mindling returned within twenty minutes. By then, mom had re-entered the waiting room too, and the other three occupants had left. The man turned out to be a godsend. He set up tests for Danny to be evaluated that same day—which went into the night, of course—a feat only a truly caring doctor could accomplish. And while he found nothing abnormal physiologically, he ultimately diagnosed Danny with PTSD. Dr. Mindling scheduled follow-up appointments for him as well, and a doctor by the name of Goldsmith prescribed him a low dose of Prozac for his nerves.

Danny felt free and light when he and his mom left Mannor Hospital. Dark, heavy chains had been lifted from his body, his heart, his mind. They'd been reduced to granulated piles of rust he didn't have to brood over anymore. Grandma Crowley was dead, and the visions had simply been a lingering phantasm created by his overactive imagination. That was it. At fourteen, the sight of a dead body—especially a loved one—had been too much. There was nothing to worry about anymore, except for maybe what flavor of ice cream to get when they drove past Dairy Fairy on the way back home.

He ended up getting chocolate. And, when he and his mom returned home, he took his medication, curious to know how it'd make him feel.

An hour later: tired. He was ready for bed at 9:30. He felt so well, his mind clean, his heart clear. Dad checked up on him, but Danny told him he was much better and needed some rest. Mom whistled while she did dishes in the kitchen. Minutes later, her whistling faded into silence, and all light, to dark.

Danny's slumber was uninterrupted by dreams and nightmarish

visions alike.

He got up bright and early the next morning, had breakfast, went to school, dished it out, and met Randy Wayde at Piker's Hill. Piker's Hill was located five miles south of Ducougery Junior High and about three miles northeast of Tinney Lane, home. Most teenagers went up there to neck. Most children went up there to enjoy the panoramic view of Ducougery. It wasn't unusual to hear explosions from the herbal side of town, as one eccentric local was rumored to have a fascination with low explosives—but he didn't bother anybody and hardly anyone ever saw him.

Randy had told Danny to expect a cool, righteous surprise when he met up with him. When Danny insisted he tell him what the surprise consisted of, Randy pretended to zip his lip.

Danny spent most of the school day wondering what Randy had to show him.

He stood at the apex of Piker's Hill for fifteen or twenty minutes, taking in the pleasant view of the town below. One could see everything from up here. His house stood somewhere toward the right, but, from this far away, among all the touting signs, seeing it was nigh impossible. McDonald's golden arches towered over the giant plastic tire that marked Luik's Tire World. Kappler's, a car-washing station not half a mile distant, whirred noisily as it power-sprayed vehicles. People looked like ants as they walked the streets. Sunlight gleamed off car windshields, casting blinding beams in different directions. Hills surrounded the general vicinity of town, and the clear-blue skies stretched on forever.

Danny stood there, hot, sweaty and alone, waving away gnats that swam about the air. A thought occurred to Danny just then, one that made him smile. *Now would be the opportune time for Grandma Crowley to show herself, because I'm all by myself, in the middle of nowhere, without anyone around for miles.*

That was not entirely true, however.

His humorous thought turned into electric horror when he heard someone bellow, *"Booo!"*

Danny jumped—literally jumped straight up off the gravel flat. Laughter followed, a familiar sort from somebody he was expecting.

"I just scared the life outta you!" Randy cried, bent over and guffawing. Danny had turned around with little memory of doing so, partly angry but mostly amused.

"Okay, Randy, it was funny. Now you promised me a surprise I'd never guess. I'm waiting. Is it an early birthday present?"

Randy stopped laughing. "No. It's a present for me—more of like a borrow from my dad. Except that he doesn't know it's missing from his bureau at the moment."

"Okay. Show me, show me!"

Randy pulled it carefully out of his book-bag. Danny's eyes bulged and dried a little in the stuffy air.

"My dad's .357 mag. A powerful sonofagun."

"Literally! Wow!"

"Yeah. Careful, it's a little heavy."

Danny gingerly took the weapon out of Randy's hands—it was heavy. Danny had played with cap guns before, but had no idea the real thing weighed as much as it did. Sunlight gleamed off its metallic finish. It had a black rubber grip, and *Smith and Wesson* stenciled across its side.

"Got bullets in it?" Danny asked him.

"Yep. I figured we could shoot some trees or stumps or something."

"Oh, man, this is awesome."

"Here, give it back a sec."

Danny set it in his open hands, being careful to aim the barrel at the ground while doing so. Randy flicked off the safety catch and cocked it with one hard, quick pull—*chick-chick!* "It's ready to fire now, man! Come on, this way."

Danny followed him into the woods. Randy led the way,

walking like he knew exactly where he was going. The boys had explored these parts many times before, so it was not new territory for him at all. There were several small abandoned campsites down this way, cluttered with far too much litter—especially beer cans.

They walked downhill on a slant, through heavy, stuffy underbrush, toward the dirt flat. It made sense that that's where Randy was leading, for the flat was the perfect spot to fire a real gun. Plus, it was heavily-shaded by vegetation.

Randy smacked at a bug or two. Danny did the same. A soft, pleasant wind ruffled shrubbery, wavered goldenrod, presenting a moment's coolness to this otherwise sweltering oven.

They stepped onto the dirt flat at 4:07. Danny glanced absently at his watch when they did, meanwhile smacking at another annoying mosquito. Randy set down his book-bag. Danny watched him aim the revolver down a long hill. The flat was roughly twenty by thirty feet, the ground covered with four-wheeler tracks and garbage.

"You ever shoot a gun before?" Danny blared enthusiastically.

"Nope, my first time, too."

"Well, what are you waiting for?"

Randy aimed at an empty bottle of vodka poking out of the dirt. Danny took a step back and waited for the big bang by cupping his hands over his ears.

The report was louder than Danny anticipated, quick and *thudding,* making him jump a little. The sound echoed through the woods like a resonant voice over a cliff. The gun kicked back quite a bit—any more and it would've probably cracked Randy in the face. The bullet missed the glass bottle, but dry dirt flew with the consistency of snow.

"Whoa." Randy smiled mischievously. "I feel like Superman with this thing in my hand."

"It's powerful."

"Damn right it is."

He aimed again. Fired again. Danny jumped again. This bang seemed louder than the last, but Danny was slightly closer. The gun almost flew back out of Randy's hand.

More dirt... no broken bottle.

"You wanna try it?" Randy asked.

Danny stepped forward, smiling stupidly, his nerves jingling in his legs and his shaking arms.

"It's not gonna bite you. Just don't hold it like me. Both hands, one over the other. That's how I watched my dad do it. That's how they do it in action movies."

Gun switched hands. These ones were two sizes smaller. The .357 felt like it weighed ten pounds to Danny as he aimed, his left leg shaking beneath him, forehead beading sweat, arms wobbling.

"Like I said," Randy repeated, "it's not gonna hurt you. Aim careful. Breathe. Let go of all that tension; you don't need it. You're the master of the gun; the gun isn't the master of you."

But Danny had trouble relaxing. He wasn't able to stop shaking. Without really thinking, he pulled the trigger while still trying to aim at the target: the vodka bottle. *BANG!* The gun jerked in his hands, but not too much—surely not as violently as he'd expected it to—and a wisp of smoke shot out of the barrel. The bottle exploded. Particles of glass filled the sun-dappled air like clear, atomized glitter.

"All right!" Randy hollered. "A natural, man, a natural. Good shootin', Dan!"

"That wasn't half as bad as I thought it was gonna be!"

"See? And you worked yourself up for nothing. Next time, I bet you won't be near as nervous."

"Can I go again?"

"Sure. Just a couple more, because I want to shoot again. There's not many left in the chamber. I didn't want to search for more ammo, and didn't want to tear apart his room looking for the cleaning kit. Dad keeps this thing cleaner than a nun's you-know-what. He says that the barrel gets dirty quick with gunpowder residue. I'm not about to tempt fate and have him find it all caked on the inside, although imagining this awesome piece of machinery blowing up in his face does sound good."

Danny laughed. More wind blew through the trees, swaying them, moving sun-dapples back and forth across the littered dirt flat. He wrapped his finger around the hard steel trigger and squeezed. His arms and legs were still. His breathing slowed. His nervousness had turned to tranquility.

He aimed at a beer can and squeezed, squeezed, squeezed.

Not afraid of this thing anymore! I know I can handle it!

The gun barked fire. The bullet missed its mark and tore through a small, rotting tree stump in the distance.

"Here ya go," Danny said, handing the gun back to Randy.

"Should be three shots left. Would you go over and set a few of those beer cans up on that log?"

Danny smiled. "Make sure you don't point that at me or nothing."

"I won't, man. Promise."

Danny walked across the dirt flat toward the heaping mounds of trash. Bending down, he picked up three beers cans very reluctantly with the tips of his fingers, careful not to touch the openings. He placed the cans, which were crumpled, on top of a fallen log. Then he turned back around.

"Randy, what are you doing, man?"

The business end of the gun was facing Danny. His heart seemed to stop.

"We're having fun, that's all. Do you think you can dodge a bullet?"

Danny thought he could see into that black hole from this distance—a tiny round hole which led to a bigger square one at Lancing Cemetery. Would he hear it go off? Would he see a flash of light before impact? Would it hurt? Would he feel it going in and coming out? Would his brains splatter on the tree behind him?

"Come on, man, why are you aiming that at me?"

Randy shrugged nonchalantly with one shoulder. "How about put one of those cans on top of your head; see if I can knock it off."

"You're scaring me."

Randy showed no emotion; his eyes were cold and dull; his mouth was taut and almost nonexistent. His finger wrapped around the trigger.

Danny turtled up, hunching his shoulders, tightening his head, waiting to die and asking why his best friend, his only friend, wanted to kill him.

"Please, man, Randy, don't do this. Quit aiming that thing at me—it could go off."

"What, afraid to die? It could go off, yeah, and it will."

Danny took a small step back, fully shelling up. He physically couldn't move his body any more after that; his muscles had locked. Another soft breeze whirred through the surrounding foliage, moving sun-dapples once again across the trash-covered ground. It looked surreal in his eyes.

Randy's eyes went from dull to sharp, and his thin-lined mouth broadened into a malicious little smirk. "Say good-bye, man."

"No! No, please! Wait!" Danny somehow managed to hold his hands up, as if they actually had the power to stop a bullet.

The sounds that followed were neither loud nor dramatic, but there were two of them—and they were both identical.

Click-click!

Randy aimed the gun to his own head and pulled the trigger a third time: *Click!* "Psych! It's empty now. What, you actually thought I was gonna shoot you?"

Danny didn't know how to feel. Angry? Scared? Confused? A multitude of emotions tunneled through him, jumping from one to the next the way a frog might jump from stone to stone across a stream. They repeated, circling around this fourteen-year-old airport, until suddenly, they stopped. Fury remained. Fury mixed with a helping of disappointment.

"Why would you do that?" He made sure to raise his voice.

Randy took a tentative step backward and lowered the gun, unable to look Danny in the eye. "Sorry." It sounded like an authentic apology, but after everything Danny had been through during the last couple of days, this was the straw that broke the camel's back. It was his turn to vent.

"Bullcrap! That was a really mean thing to do, and I'm not gonna stand for it." Danny kicked the cans off the log. He marched away, shoulder-bumping Randy as he went, his breaths short, shallow, and raging. Randy tried grabbing hold of his arm, but Danny was having none of it. He hurried away, crying, his heart tender and red. "I'm going home. Don't follow me."

"I didn't know, man, I'm sorry. It was a joke."

"Piss-poor idea of a joke."

"Don't go, Danny. Do you hate me now? I don't.... have any other... you're my only friend!"

Danny ran. He ran out of the woods, down a long hill, and into town. Though it took roughly twenty minutes to get home from this point on, he made it in eighteen.

He slammed the front door behind him, rattling a mirror hanging from the wall in the hallway. His mom, who was sitting on the couch in the living room, asked him what was wrong.

"Nothing!"

"Did you have another—"

He knew what she was going to say before she said it: *Did you have another vision of Grandma? Was she there at school again? Oh, it's okay, it's not real, I won't let nothing hurt you, you know that?*

Danny went to his room. He slammed that door, too, got into bed, and cried, unsure of why he was doing so. Because of Randy's little stunt or because of everything else, he didn't know, he just needed to get it all out.

Danny didn't eat supper that night. His mom called for him, but he didn't answer. When dad knocked on his door, he told him to go away. He wanted to forget about today, about Randy, about the last few days, and just hibernate.

In fact, he wanted to know what it felt like to be emotionally alone, separated from fear, from anger, from confusion, from all human emotions, and feel completely, unequivocally numb.

He lay there until nightfall, hands laced behind head, thinking, pondering, and wondering, before a real stint of numbness fell over him.

At 11:47 he was ready to go to sleep. He'd taken his medication earlier today, before school, and was not concerned about Grandma Crowley or her black goat of a thousand young or whatever else his wounded imagination was capable of conjuring up.

He had nothing to worry about... until 3:00 a.m. came trundling along.

Though locked firmly in deep, comfortable sleep, Danny suddenly woke up, removed from that tranquil numbness he so desperately wanted, by a presence he couldn't understand or comprehend. His eyes opened as if the lids had been removed. He couldn't move, couldn't speak, couldn't do anything but be a witness to the dark.

What is happening?

He knew. He knew well, he just didn't want to accept it.

Grandma...

His eyes flitted around the room, found nothing out of the ordinary, and stopped on the desk to his left. The bottle of medication stood on the corner of it. He tried reaching, to get his motor functions to obey, but they did not. *Pills will make all this go away. I'll go back to sleep. This nightmare will fade into darkness. All be all right.*

Why can't I move?

He'd received his wish—numbness throughout his entire body. There was no feeling in his limbs or anywhere else other than his eyes, which were dry and hot. It was as though someone—

Grandma?—had injected every nerve with the kind of novocaine dentists used. Yet, his eyes refused to close, even a little. The sensation was weird, the epitome of true powerlessness of the human will. He was a living mummy at the moment, hopefully not forever.

Speaking was an exercise in futility, as well, for his lips refused to function. Along with his eyes, his brain still worked, his heart still worked, chugging along, his adrenaline spilling liquid terror through his veins at Mach 5. He looked for her, Evil Ethel, all the while telling himself that this was just a night terror.

There was movement at the foot of his bed. Movement that came from the ground up. She rose slowly from beneath his listless feet, emerging like a lackadaisical whack-a-mole from its dark cavern. Her white hair moved with sentient purpose, the horns already protruding through her sunken temples. Face draped in black shadow, she stood with her hands clasped together. She revealed herself, her despicable silhouette, which light didn't seem to want to cast its beauty on.

"Danny boy, oh Danny!" she whispered in that grotesque, chronic-smoker's voice that sounded too resonate in tone. He thought his eyes were widening. "Danny, you fouled him. You blabbed and told others. We can't have that now, can we? Does granny need to watch you more closely? Not completely in my power, not yet, but I can, and will, monitor you, oh yes!"

Not real not real not real!

And just like that, she was gone...

Though he was still unable to move, her sudden reappearance rocked something vital within him—perhaps his soul. She now stood crouched beside his bed, looking down at him, her face only a foot away. This time, his eyes caught a profound glimpse of her in all her stark grotesqueness, and he knew his bladder let go. The sight jarred him to the bone, to the core, into the deepest recesses of his psyche.

Her empty, foul-smelling eye sockets oozed a yellow pus and

ran with blackened blood. The hundreds of wrinkles that lined her face were so deep, so distinct, they looked like gashes. Bugs crawled from nostril to nostril; both ears fell off and turned to dust upon contact with the floor. The ram-like horns, sharp-looking and covered with gray matter, were rimmed with glimmering rings of gold. Her chin protruded. Moles appeared and grew and burst in mucky splatters. But, despite all those things, it was her mouth that frightened Danny most. It stretched to where the lobes of her twisted ears should've been, opened before his very eyes. Teeth were missing. The tongue elongated and split in two down the center. And through several holes in her black, ruddy gums, baby fingers emerged and wiggled frantically around. Dozens of them. The horrific vision was made worse by the wails of children trapped deep inside that bottomless mouth, screaming for help, for someone to free their trapped souls. It overwhelmed Danny, throwing his mind into a dizzying spin. Awareness began to sail away when Ethel Crowley lastly pricked his arm in the same spot nurses did when they took your blood.

"The black goat of a thousand young is coming, Danny. The stars are forming in alliance to the Zodiac! It was no coincidence that I died days ago. It was meant to be. This is meant to be! I thank you for this. Our mission is approaching completion, Grandson."

Danny flew upright in bed the next morning and emitted the most gut-wrenching scream. His parents hurried into the room long before he was able to gain his bearings. Mom was shaking. Dad's mouth stood ajar.

"What is it, baby?" Mom mumbled. "Grandma dream?"

Danny shook his head. "Not a dream, Mom. She's not a dream. This *is* real."

"Where are your meds?" she asked.

Danny followed her gaze to the stand. The pill bottle was not were it had been last night. Dad marched over and checked to see if it had fallen on the floor. "I don't see it. Do you know where it went, Dan—what's that smell?"

Danny threw the blankets aside, revealing a large yellow stain on the sheets below his groin. Mom gasped. Dad furrowed his brows and said, "I know what you two told me, but could you go into detail? A lot more detail on this matter?"

Mom shook her head—whipped her head. "I don't... I don't know." She looked and sounded genuinely scared. "Are you okay, Danny?"

"No! No, I'm not. This is all getting worse."

"Danny, come on, don't talk to your mother that way."

"Then tell me how to talk, *Daaad!* If either of you two saw what I saw last night, you'd be... I can't do this."

"And you won't," Dad snapped. "Those pills surely made you worse. You're obviously not getting better, but I ain't gonna have to buy you new sheets and a new mattress every few days. We're dealing with this now, today."

Mom gave dad a reproachful look. "David, he's terrified. Be easy on him."

"Be easy on him? When he's yelling at you? At me? Being smart? Ruining these?" He lifted up a corner of the bed sheet. "I'm not gonna have it, Amy, and neither should you."

"Fine." She waved a hand at him.

"What are you getting mad at me for? I'm sticking up for you!"

"I don't need you sticking up for me, *David. God!*"

Danny didn't want this. He didn't want any of this. His heart was breaking and the burden was too much to bear.

"Stop it! Stop it! Stop it! I'll move out into some gutter and leave you alone. I won't worry you into a nervous breakdown, Mom. I won't destroy your precious laundry, Dad. I'll go and let Grandma Crowley do whatever she wants, whatever that is. I'll be gone, and things'll be fine again. Okay? Sound good?"

His parents refused to look at each other—and at him. He got up out of bed, fuming, brushed past his mom, and padded into the hall.

"Danny," she cried, "where are you going? Where are you going, Danny *Ray* Willow!"

He'd made it to the top of the staircase when he heard her pronounce his middle name. He stopped and turned, looking back.

"What, Mother?"

She stumbled a little, obviously hurt. "What is wrong with you?"

"What's wrong with me is that grandma, your mom, is some kind of demon who's after me. That's what's wrong. What's also wrong is this: nobody believes me. Everybody thinks it's my imagination. I wish it was, trust me, but it's not."

He turned back around, ready to leave for school or Antarctica or Mars—anywhere to escape this problem.

"Danny Ray Willow!" she called again.

He stopped, but didn't turn. "Yeah?"

"Where are you going?"

He turned around and replied, solemnly, "I don't know. I don't know."

"I'm willing to believe you. Please don't leave. We'll help you. Dad and I will help you."

"Willing isn't enough, Mom. I'm going to school."

"You can stay home, if you like."

Dad protested, "Are you crazy too? What are you saying?"

"What about breakfast?" Her voice quivered. "Can't you—"

Against his better judgment, he left. He was out the door and marching down his driveway when he heard the sobs of his heartbroken mother through the second-story window. He was on the verge of tears himself as he ran east along Tinney Lane, then west down Carson, destination: Piker's Hill.

He almost got hit by a car on Harper Street. The tan Sudan seemed to come out of nowhere, screeching to a stop just inches from his waist. The driver, a wiry-looking long-haired man with a short temper, pressed in on his horn for a good ten seconds. Danny gave him a dirty look. The man responded by giving him the middle finger before speeding off. *More of what I need.* From that point on, Danny reached Piker's Hill without incident, where he, once again, took in the beautiful sight of Ducougery.

It didn't look like the place he knew—didn't *feel* like the place he knew. That was normal though, wasn't it? You could look at the same exact thing several times and always see something different. Emotion played the most vital role in what one perceived. Where one person saw significant beauty, another might see pure ugliness. It wasn't just in the eye of the bolder; it was also dependent upon the viewer's mind at each given moment.

He felt like he was stuck in a state of disrepair. Where was he to go from here? Nobody believed him. He had enough trouble believing it himself. He understood everyone's doubt. His old, dead hag of a grandmother was after him, and he had little time left. What would happen on that last day, or night? He didn't *really* want to find out, despite the curiosity. What he needed more than anything was unbridled proof. Something to show everyone so that they would, without a doubt, take him seriously. So how was he to do that?

The air was still and dead on Piker's Hill, as if the entire world had simply.... stopped. Danny stood there crying, mourning his own life that he would never get to live out. He actually felt Death perched on his shoulders, pushing him down, crushing his insides flat. These were probably the same type of emotions one would have when faced with their own mortality after a doctor told them, "Oh, I'm sorry, you've only got months to live."

Only, in his case, he had days.

And he was only fourteen.

And the actual diagnosis was unclear.

"Please, Ethel Crowley," he said, looking up at the sky, the unmoving horizon, "Please leave me alone. I don't want to die. Why are you doing this to me, huh? What did I ever do to you? What did I ever do to you..."

He wiped away some tears. His nose was full of snot. The

crying felt good, anyhow, relieving.

Then he asked the question of questions. "What are you? What have you become?"

Despite a lack of wind, the nearby shrubs that lined the entrance to the woods, rattled. Danny turned, looking through his blurry, tear-filled eyes. *Something's hiding, watching.* Whatever it was had some mass to it, too.

"Show yourself, you no-good, evil witch."

That's it, Danny, piss her off. Make her do worse to you.

The bushes shook again, harder, noisily.

He took a few steps back. "What do you want from me? What do you really want? Why can't you just leave me alone? I don't—"

What came out of the bushes wasn't some monstrous evil or a black goat of a thousand young. Instead, it was a dog, a Jack Russel Terrier.

Danny knelt down and extended his hand. The dog walked over, tail wagging from side to side, smiling affectionately with its canines. Its earnest friendliness upset some of the darkness permeating inside of him, and he let that go. Some of it actually went away.

He was smiling, the dog was smiling, and he was petting it, and it was gladly accepting all his attention. It licked his face with its long, rough, wet tongue. Every kiss burned away tension and angst. It scratched at his arms, as if saying, *keep going, keep petting, I'll be your best friend.* This dog, in his mind, was everything his grandmother wasn't.

The dog jumped up, lying its front paws on his shoulder. He hugged the Jack Russel back, feeling all the love and warmth it had to offer.

"Are you lost, buddy?" Danny checked for a collar. He found it: Lolly Jinkens, 555-3106. He also noticed some scratches on its neck—probably caused by a run-in with another animal. "You okay, Lolly? Looks like you got in a fight or something. I wish I could mend your wounds, but they don't look too bad. I think they'll heal up pretty quick. You're a good doggy, you know that?"

The dog flashed another smile. Danny smiled back and scratched Lolly's head some more.

"Come on, I'll help you find your way home. Would you like that?"

Lolly barked playfully at him. Then it nudged his left arm with its paw. Danny felt a twinge of pain there, so he examined the crook of his elbow. It looked like it had been pricked by something –maybe a needle. The sore looked gnarly and was filled with pus.

"What the... how did I get that?"

The pain hadn't existed until Lolly had scratched at it, and when he looked down at her, she barked twice, tail-wagging, panting. Danny took this as confirmation, that the lesion wasn't just random, but put there deliberately...

By Grandma Crowley?

It was possible. And, as he thought back, struggling to piece together last night's events, he remembered being pinched shortly before passing out.

She did this to me. I got proof now.

Hold up, Skippy. This isn't proof of anything; this is a pinprick you could have gotten from anywhere, anyhow. Nobody's going to connect this to the supernatural, and I probably wouldn't if I was in the same boat, either.

If Ethel had put it there, that meant one of two things: either she had extracted something from him or had injected something into him. If so, what? What was it doing in him? More importantly, what was it doing to him? Was it killing him? Floating through his bloodstream, a bug that'd kill him in several days?

She said something when she did it—I remember that. She told me what she was doing, and what it would do.

Think, stupid, think!

But he was too close to the material. So close that he couldn't distinguish the words from the information. The answer eluded him, despite it being right in front of his face, staring directly at him.

He walked Lolly home, received a monetary gift for doing so from a grizzled middle-aged man out on Jamison Lane. The man thanked him half a dozen times—Danny wasn't counting, but it seemed like that many—and took Lolly, who seemed to want to follow Danny, back inside. After that, Danny walked to school, still dressed in the same ensemble as yesterday. He had no books with him, no lunch, no pens or pencils. He felt like a wanderer roaming the streets, and perhaps, in a way, that's what he was.

Then again, who wasn't? Wasn't everybody roaming the world with no knowledge of their place, their destiny, or why they were here? Why did life even exist? Had the big bang randomly prompted it? Or was there purpose behind it? A grand scheme constructed by alien beings, or God, or something else? Nobody really knew, and the fact that nobody knew may have been merciful as much as terrifying, depending on how one looked at it.

Danny didn't have all the answers; barely any, in fact. All he knew for certain was that dark, malicious forces existed. There was no doubt about that. Evil could survive after death, and could definitely consume, because that's how Danny felt whenever he thought of his grandmother. He had no idea if she could be stopped. He still had no idea *what* she was. Thankfully, maybe miraculously, last night's events were a blur. All he could remember was the pinch to his arm, and that's about it.

School had already begun by the time he got there. Mrs. Briner was none too pleased by his tardiness. Randy, on the hand, looked extremely apologetic.

"You know how I feel about students who run into my classroom forty-six—" She checked her watch. "minutes late, Mr. Willow?"

He tried keeping his eyes on the floor, but felt compelled to look at Randy, who offered the most sincere smile Danny had ever seen, in real life or on TV.

"No, Mrs. Briner," Danny replied. "I am sorry I'm late. I got things going on in my life right now."

Mrs. Briner made a stink-face and rolled her eyes. Kids laughed at him as he took his seat across from Randy.

"We don't care about your private life, Dannyboy."

"What did you say?" He was leering at Mrs. Briner now. His reply sounded like an implicit threat.

"I said, we don't care about your life, Danny."

He stared her down with such enmity, she took a few steps back. Her intense look crumbled. "Are you mouthing off to me, Danny? I can send you straight to the principal's office."

He shook his head. "I'm sorry, Mrs. Briner."

She cocked her head to the side and smiled at him with what could only be two immense sets of false teeth. To Danny, this frightening grimace seemed to last far too long. *Do they see it? Her weird smile? Are they seeing it too—*

He blinked his eyes. Suddenly, Mrs. Briner was standing over him, yardstick in one hand, red chalk in the other. The smiling apparition must have been visible to him alone. "Mr. Willow!" She raised her voice. "Turn to chapter three. If you hadn't been tardy, you'd know that—"

"Why don't you leave him the hell alone, you crazy cow?"

Did I hear that? Who said that? Was it real?

I don't know what's real anymore.

Every head in class turned toward the voice that Danny thought sounded like Randy's. Randy gazed at the teacher, eyes aflame. She gaped, horrified, stunned, defeated.

"What did you say to me, Mr. Wayde?" she asked tremulously.

"You heard me," Randy shot back. "You leave my friend alone. He's going through a tough time in life, and you're all over him like a vulture over roadkill."

She pointed to the door with her trusty yardstick. It convulsed in her wrinkly hand.

"Principal's office, now!"

Randy made no fuss. He got up, his attention focused more on Danny than Briner. He gave Danny a smile and an amiable nod before leaving the room. The faces of several teenagers burned bright with astonishment. Jacob was giggling. Thomas Willings had to cover his mouth with both hands in order to abstain from laughing. Justine Garrage, the prettiest girl in all of Danny's classes, looked swan-turned-toad by her reaction to this spectacle.

 Mrs. Briner held fast to her anger, smacking desk after desk with her yardstick as she walked brokenly toward the front of her class.

She turned around, in tears, and said in a defeated voice, "Today we'll learn about how light works." She didn't make eye-contact with anyone.

Danny didn't stick around for science; screw it, he was a dead kid walking, and Randy was a lot more important to him than learning about light.

He stood outside Principal Redding's room for roughly five minutes, watching Redding, a mean old square point and shout and belittle his best friend. "You're a little punk. You're never gonna amount to anything, Wayde." He tossed a file onto his desk and opened it. "Fighting. Stealing. Vandalism. Cursing. You've been in detention more often than anyone I've ever seen. Do you know that? I see your face more often than my wife's. You know what's going to come of you? I bet I can predict your life story. Easy. You're gonna end up quitting within a year or two. Your deadbeat parents are gonna die or kick you out, and you're gonna live in the streets, under overpasses, in cardboard boxes, juicing up on drugs. You're gonna steal to find that, as well as food. But food and drink won't be as important as your juice. You'll wind up in prison for awhile, get out, go back, and repeat this process. In the end, you're gonna spend your life in and out of prison, in the grave, or on the streets doing nothing because you're a filthy loser. That's the sad truth."

Danny couldn't believe his ears. Principal Redding, a tall, lanky man with a chiseled face and little hair, was upsetting him, making him cry, abusing him. Danny wasn't going to stand for it; besides, what did it matter if he got detention? He had his mortality to worry about. And a friend to save. Screw the consequences.

"Randy," he said, opening the door. "Let's get outta this hellhole. Come on."

Danny never looked at Redding during this interruption. Randy got up and hurried out of the room, and Danny slammed the door shut before the principal could do much of anything.

"Sorry you had to hear that, buddy," Danny said. "You know it's all bullcrap."

They walked outside and stood under the eaves. It had begun to do something Danny hadn't seen it do in two years—something he'd never expected to see it do so soon in the fall. Snow. It fell in thick, fluffy flakes, forming thin blankets on the ground, turning everything white—the polar opposite of how Danny felt.

"Maybe he was right," Randy said bleakly. "Maybe I will turn out to be a loser. I have thought about quitting, man, I've thought about it a lot. If I dropped out, I don't think my mom or dad would even bat their eyes."

"Lots of successful people drop out of high-school."

"But they're not losers! They're not like me. They have ambitions, goals, dreams, money, parents who care. You know my parents, I'm only good to be around if they want chores done or if they want to beat me."

Danny turned away from Randy's pitiable face. "Anyone who beats you, Randy, whether they're your parents, kids, or the principal, are much bigger losers than you are, which you're not. You're just a little messed up because your mom and dad are big-time messed up. What example do you have to follow, man?"

Randy smiled graciously. "You, Danny. You."

"And you're not gonna lose me, not even when I die in several days..." Danny caught his little slip up, and then caught his friend's wretched reaction.

"What? What do you mean, you're gonna die in several days?"

Danny didn't lift his head; he kept his eyes glued to the ground, which turned whiter and whiter. "I shouldn't tell you."

"Just tell me. I won't judge you, laugh, or anything."

You told about me, Dannyboy.

The memory walloped him. Danny looked into Randy's eyes. *I only got one shot at this, don't I?* "My dead grandma's come back from hell to take me with her."

Randy didn't do any of the things Danny expected him to. He didn't look away. He didn't smile or laugh. He didn't step back. His eyes didn't even budge. No adverse expression crossed his face. He stood there looking lamely at him.

"What do you think? Do you believe me?"

Nothing...

Then: "We're all going through something. Sometimes it's just a little bit different than everything else. And yes, I believe you. But I'd like to know more."

"I'll tell you all I can, but I know very little, and she... she warned me not to tell. That she had to monitor me or something."

"Reminds me of about a dozen science fiction movies."

"Really?"

"They implant tiny devices that record everything you do. Your actions, conversations, encounters, stuff like that."

Danny lifted his arm. Randy took it in his hands and examined the wound, as if he knew right where it was. The sore was bigger than it had been earlier on Piker's Hill. Pus was oozing out of it.

"I can't see it too well," Danny said, "because of the placement."

"That's okay. Holy crap!"

"What? What is it? What do you see?"

Danny read Randy's face. It said, without speaking, *You-gotta-be-kidding-me-this-is-freaking-crazy-voodoo-stuff-I-can't-wrap-*

my-head-around.

Randy pinched his arm, inflicting pain that was fairly minimal. Danny glanced up at the white sky and stuck his tongue out, catching snowflakes on it.

"Okay," Randy said, the horror on his face worsening. "I believe you about your grandma, man, I do. And this isn't the only reason why. Take a look at this!"

Randy held up a wiggling maggot between his fingertips. Instead of being off-white, almost yellow, this maggot was black. Black and slimy and disgusting and strange.

Evidence, Danny thought, reaching for it... but Randy dropped it onto the pavement and crushed it under his big black boot.

"No, wait!"

62

Chapter Six

"Why? Randy asked.

Danny pouted, "That's the only evidence I had that would sway my parents. I needed something tangible to show others."

Randy scoffed. "Really? You think that would do it?"

"It was black. No maggots are black."

"You don't know that. There are albino alligators and all kinds of unusual things in the natural world. Why can't there be a black maggot? Something could've happened to it to make it that way. Come on, you know how adults are. They'll believe anything but the truth, because once they hit a certain age, they stop believing in *evvverything.*"

"They would've saw the hole in my arm—"

Randy rolled his eyes. "A hole which could've been caused by a million other things, reality-based things."

Danny took a breath. "What am I gonna do, man? You're the only one who believes me. And now that that maggot's dead and gone, Crowley's going to know. Tonight she might put ten of those disgusting things in my body. She's gonna be more po'ed."

"Well, from now on, you're not staying alone by yourself. I'm going to be there when you're awake and asleep. I'm going to monitor you."

"What if you don't see her? What if her magic's somehow restricted to me?"

Randy pointed at the crushed maggot on the ground. "That was real. I saw it. Maybe her presence is dependent upon the person. Like I said, when people hit a certain age, their belief in this kind thing goes away. The older you get, the more cynical you become."

Danny shook his head. "Maybe I'm just crazy."

"Hey!" Randy grabbed him by his shoulders, and they looked into each other's eyes. "You're not crazy. I'm not crazy. I pulled a freaking maggot out of your arm that was planted there by your dead grandmother. We ain't crazy, man. The psychos out there who don't believe are the crazy ones."

Danny chuckled. He let his smile stay. "You think so?"

"No. I know so!"

"You think we should go back..." Danny nodded toward the school.

"Didn't you hear? I'm a future dropout loser who's on the juice. Hell, no, I'm never going back to that place, and neither should you... until we get this all figured out. Okay?"

Danny nodded, still smiling. "Okay."

"Now let's go get something to eat. I got money. Anywhere you want. You choose, I pay. Cool? And you tell me everything that's happened so far."

Danny's smile widened. "Awesome."

Chapter Seven

Amy sat in the recliner in the living room, willing to believe her son, Danny. She wanted to, needed to, tried forcing herself to, but had trouble doing so. She sat there looking back and forth from the window to one of her favorite pictures of her Mother Ethel, with her son. The picture had been taken a good seven years ago, back when Danny was seven and Ethel was still in pretty good health. They were standing on a dock in front of the Ohio River, smiling, looking goofy, and laughing. Amy remembered Danny had said something funny that day, but couldn't remember just what.

Snow fell outside, coming down hard, and Amy just watched it without seeing it. She'd been crying for awhile. David had gone to work nearly an hour ago, and she had the house all to herself. She'd thought about phoning school a few times, just to make sure Danny had made it, but stopped herself. She needed to think.

Had there been a time, ever in her past, when Ethel had done something odd, out of the ordinary?

She felt there had, at least once, once in all the time she'd known her mother. Where this memory was stored and how she could access it, however, remained a mystery.

Danny needed to be believed. He needed to be heard. She was willing, willing to give her life for his, in fact, and do anything that would make him well again.

It was just too difficult to believe that Ethel had come back from the dead, though. If she'd come back, she would've embraced him, told him she was all right, in better place, not returned with the fury of hell.

No, Danny was sick. He had to be mentally ill. Besides, he was at the right age to experience hallucinations caused by the onset of schizophrenia—but that was another thing. Ailments like that didn't run in her family. Or David's.

What is reality, she asked herself, watching snow fall without processing it. She glanced back at the photograph, and her eyes focused carefully on Ethel. That's when her mind turned over and something inside clicked. A long-forgotten memory crawled to the surface like a mole burrowing a tunnel up through the ground. It cropped up quickly, from the deepest depths of her subconscious, one she'd obviously filed in a cabinet labeled, NOT VERY IMPORTANT.

She had been eleven, twelve, thirteen—somewhere in that age range. Ethel had been nearing her seventies. This was long after dad had passed from an unbeknownst illness the doctors couldn't identify. It had been late in the night—this detail stood out strong and well—and Amy had been unable to fall asleep. So she watched a little TV and ate some ice cream, when she heard a noise from upstairs. Sounded like a groan from an old, old woman.

Amy got up, walked past a picture window that overlooked the front yard, and made her way to the back wall, behind which a set of thirteen steps led up to a door at the top. Ethel's room.

Light penetrated the cracks of the closed door—soft, flickering orange illumination that could only be the glimmer of candles. Amy climbed the stairs, unsure if she should be snooping... or disturbing her mother, who could be sleeping... She climbed, dragged upwards by childlike curiosity, toward the large door at the top.

She grabbed the brass knob, turned it, pushed, and entered. Burning candles illuminated the room in an eerie glow of gentle, but somehow old-fashioned, light. They looked strategically placed, set up in odd yet careful patterns atop a table, which also had an air of an antiquity about it. In fact, everything in the room had that old-world vibe to it—the walls, the stands, the bed, the vanity. Every structural piece of wood in the room looked as though it had been cut from trees centuries past. But, given that she had come up in an earlier time, that was probably normal.

But Ethel wasn't sleeping; she wasn't even in bed. She was

sitting at the head of the table, between it and the southeast window that overlooked the road. It wasn't Ethel's sitting there that dismayed Amy; it was the fact that she was sitting so perfectly still. It was the fact that Ethel's eyes were rolled back inside her head, glassy and sightless. It was also the fact that there was a chunk of quartz crystal sitting on the table in front of her.

Amy opened her mouth to speak, curiosity brimming, and walked over to see if her mother was all right. Not only were her eyes wholly sclera, her body stiff and rigid, her mind seemingly gone, but her butt was not even in the chair. It wasn't touching it. It hovered a foot over the seat. Ethel was levitating, levitating in thin air, oblivious to the world around her. And when the candles flickered and the quartz crystal glowed a dull pink color, Annie went running out of the room, padding down the steps and back to her room, shaken up.

How could I have forgotten that? Something so weird, so unbelievable. That's a memory that should've remained fresh and important. My mother had levitated, and I couldn't remember for that many decades?

Or maybe, Amy thought, she had suppressed the memory for the simplest reason of all—to forget. To quell any kind of unnecessary fear, to honor her mother's good name and not some crazy notion that she, Ethel, had a lot more going on than she, Amy, wanted to acknowledge.

Her willingness to believe her son, after this emergence, was now turning to hard realization. Of course, that memory could've been just an old, forgotten dream, but she doubted it. It felt real. It seemed real. *What's real and what's imagined are sometimes two unclear things when you are a kid of the age of eleven, twelve, or thirteen.*

You didn't recognize the blatant difference until you became a cynical adult, somewhere around the age of twenty—at least for her.

So she sat there for minutes, hours, mulling, worrying—the

curse of a good mother, watching snow fall through dull, sightless eyes of her own, wondering if her mother had dabbled in the occult during her living days, and if her son was really, truly telling the God-honest truth.

Chapter Eight

The local Dairy Queen stood on the corner of Hilman Street, near the southeast end of town. It had partition windows that overlooked one of the busiest roads in Ducougery: the Hilman-Turner intersection. Wrecks happened here all the time because of a poorly-calculated lay-out. Stop signs were easier and cheaper than lights, for one thing; for another, the roads were too narrow and always needed fixing. Motorists liked to avoid murdering their tires on rough terrain, even if that meant rear-ending or T-boning somebody in the process.

Danny and Randy sat in a booth by the slanted partition windows in Dairy Queen, eating Blizzards and watching snow fall. Danny asked himself if this was the last time he would see such beautiful precipitation, because who knew what the days ahead entailed.

"You all right?" Randy asked him.

"No." Danny laughed nervously. He ate of spoonful of Mint Chocolate chip. Cold goodness swam into his stomach.

"Don't worry," Randy consoled.

"Don't worry? That's all I'm doing. I don't know if it's the stress of it, but I feel like death. I feel it everywhere, everywhere I go, everything I look it—it all makes me feel blacker inside. I don't know how else to explain it."

"That's how I feel all the time when I'm at home." Randy shoved some Oreo Blizzard into his mouth. His throat bobbed as he swallowed. "I ask myself, what kind of mood is dad going to be in today? Is he going to have one of his good days where he leaves me alone? Or is he going to have one of his bad days where he gets physical? The beatings never get easier. While he's doing it, I feel that presence of death, too. Sometimes the thought's there that... what if he sends me to the hospital? Or worse? You know? I want to run away, man, that's all I wanna do. Get a part-time job, save up, and get the hell out. Your demon's your dead grandmother; mine's my living father. And there are other times when I wish he'd kill me just so I won't have to deal with it anymore."

Danny was at a loss for words. He'd known things were bad for Randy for some time, but not on what level, because Randy rarely mentioned the issue and Danny was not bold enough to pry. Now that he knew, he felt closer to his friend.

"Why don't we?" Randy asked, stirring his blizzard with his red plastic spoon. "Just leave, go somewhere, any place but here?"

Sounded marvelous to Danny, but no matter where he went, he figured Grandma Crowley would follow. Either way, he'd always be looking over his shoulder for the rest of his life. Who knew how long that would be?

"We can't run away from our problems. Believe me, I'd love to. But I can't carry this burden with me any longer, anywhere I go. I'd go crazy just the same."

Randy ate the rest of his Blizzard. It was runny by now. "True. We gotta face our demons to conquer, not retreat, right?"

"I wasn't trying to be so philosophical, but yeah, I guess. And who knows? I could travel halfway across the world and she might be there. My moving would be all in vain."

"Yeah, with my luck, I'd probably get in trouble with the law or hook up with some girl crazier than me."

"You're not crazy," Danny countered. "You're damaged goods."

"And you're not seeing things. You're really possessed. What do you think she is? Why do you think she's after you?"

Danny shrugged and ate the last of his Blizzard. The minty aftertaste was exquisite. He looked out the window and watched snow fall in a blizzard of its own. "I have no idea, man. I don't know. But I need to find out fast."

Randy nodded, staring at him. "So, we search. We go to the house she was in—the one your Uncle Lanny lives in now, right?"

"Yeah." Danny nodded and wiped his mouth with a napkin. His belly felt full, but his gut felt empty. "Would you spend the night with me there? Lanny's offered to have me stay the night. I think he'll be cool if I invite you too. Can't hurt."

Randy smiled. "And one of us looks around while the other distracts him?"

"I think it's an okay idea. I mean, I don't have many other options. There's gotta be something in that room of hers, something that'll tell us more about who she is... considering it's still there and my uncle didn't throw anything out yet. I don't think he will, though; he and my grandma were both kinda pack rats."

"When should we do this?" Randy asked enthusiastically.

"I'll ask him tonight. Will you ask your parents if you can stay over my house?"

"I will. And if they say no, I'll be there anyways. I'm here for you, man, through thick and thin. You're like my brother, the only person I can count on. So you can count on me."

They held hands for a brief minute, then watched the snow come down some more. The boys took it in, two broken souls seeking whatever comfort they could get—even if it was as small and frivolous as a wintry sight.

Chapter Nine

They left Dairy Queen at twenty after two in the afternoon. The air was chill, the wind like a battering ram. The thought struck Danny: *Is Grandma somehow behind this too?*

He followed Randy down a walkway and past a row of shrubs, toward the wind, which bit them like invisible claws. At least an inch of snow covered the ground now; it gritted under their shoes, sounding soft and inviting to Danny. A car beeped in the distance. A dog barked closer in.

They walked down six concrete steps to the sidewalk below. Then they walked past the serics of partition windows they'd been looking out of minutes ago. Snow was beginning to obscure any view of the inside. Cars whooshed past them on the opposite side, some carrying the pungent stench of cigarette smoke.

The pastel gray sky made Ducougery look old and relinquished as they walked down Hilman Street. Danny thought about his Uncle Lanny, and whether he'd allow Randy to spend the night, and ultimately doubted he would. But it was imperative. It had to be done, because they had to find out what kind of monster Ethel Crowley really was. Was she even human? Who was she? What was she? He also remembered her mentioning something about... obtaining the power of demons? What did that mean? Did Ethel Crowley have the power of demons? If so, how had she attained this power? Why had she conjured these entities in the first place?

More questions, less answers. These were things he, with Randy's help, was determined to unearth. So what if Lanny flat-out told him, *No, absolutely not. He can't stay*? Teenagers had been rebelling against adults since the beginning of time. Danny would try using his charm first, at least, but if that didn't work, he'd sneak Randy into the house. And if Crowley attempted to foil this scheme, so what? It was worth a try. Anything was worth trying when you had just days left to live. Anything.

They walked west down Ashland Boulevard, a side street that led to several narrow alleyways and dead-ends. The cold persisted, as did the snow. Then, for no reason, Randy stopped in his tracks. He almost slipped.

"Oh no, oh God, no."

"What?" Danny cried, his heart leaping. "What is it?" But he saw what Randy did just seconds later: Jack. Randy's dad sat behind the wheel of a rusted Cadillac, swerving, a bottle of beer gripped in his left hand. His eyes were red with fury—his pudgy face very near the same shade—and zoned in on his boy like a heat-seeking missile. Randy halted, unsure what to do, where to go. Danny surmised that he considered running by the awkward way he shifted his weight from one foot to the other.

Jack actually righted the car into the correct lane, barreling in. He chugged the rest of his beer the way a dehydrated man might chug a canteen of water in the desert. Then he threw the bottle out the window. It landed on the sidewalk, where it bounced and rolled, unbroken by the soft blanket of snow. The Cadillac trundled toward Randy, speeding up, slowing down, swerving again. Randy froze. He froze where he stood, unable to move.

Jack looked enraged, homicidal. He never so much as glanced at the road; Randy was the sole target in his cross-hairs.

"Take off, man," Danny told him. "Let's go through this alley here." Danny pointed down the nearest alley, between a set of old railroad tracks and some abandoned buildings.

Randy thought about it—Danny could see it in his eyes. He wanted to run, might have even tried to... but the madman behind the wheel had him caught like a fly in a spider's web.

"Come on, Randy." Danny grabbed his wrist, but Randy wrenched his arm out of his grip.

"I can't."

"Why? We gotta get out of here, or else both of us are in deep."

"If I go, I'll get it worse. Can't run away from our problems, remember? Demons follow, and the longer your outrun them, the worse it gets when they do find you."

Randy stopped bouncing from foot to foot. His shoulders slumped, and his head lolled a little as his dad pulled up to him. Randy turned away. Danny steeled himself and forced himself to look at Jack, who seemed to refuse to acknowledge him.

"I getta call from your principal, you little no-good bum of a son, and see you out roaming the streets when you should be in school, in detention *again,* mouthing of teachers? That does it." His words were so badly slurred, Danny could barely make them out. He wondered, *if he was this drunk when he left home, considering he came from there, how did he make it here on all the snow-covered streets from Larson Ridge? Without wrecking?* That was impressive.

"Sorry, Dad. I'm so sorry. Please—"

Jack got out of the car, stumbling onto the sidewalk, and clutched Randy's arm so forcibly it looked like it hurt. Randy winced. His face turned the color of raw meat. Jack's ugly mug turned a brighter shade of crimson. Snow was turning everything into a winter wonderland—except for these two blushers, one who was virtually mad, the other who was downright petrified.

Jack tried forcing Randy into the backseat. When Randy refused to get in by grabbing onto the Cadillac's door frame, Jack cracked him in the face with his fist.

"Hey, don't you hit him!" Danny cried, his insides boiling with anger.

"You get the hell outta here, you little troublemaker. You're no good for my loser kid. He don't need friends like you. And you're not gonna see him again. I guarantee that."

"What are you gonna do to him?" Danny shot back.

"It's none of your damn business and never was. Go home!"

Danny exploded. Something inside him gave way, and suddenly he didn't care about size, about pain, about fear, about anything. He loved Randy more in this moment than ever before, and wasn't going to let a drunken middle-aged bully hurt his friend. Not if he had anything to do with it.

Danny went to open the door to the backseat, but Jack pushed him away. "You get gone, kid! He's not your worry. If I ever see yins together again, I'm gonna call de cops on you myself. You're not to call, not to come around. Get lost!"

Regardless, Danny tried to open the door again, to do what he could to free Randy, but Jack managed to push and nudge him away.

"Stop it!" he screamed, finally looking down at Danny. Danny realized he wasn't struggling with a man; he was struggling with a 250-pound robot fueled by alcohol. You couldn't reason with someone like that.

"You let him go!" Danny screamed, his face reddening.

Jack ignored him and got back into the driver's seat. Meanwhile, Randy looked at Danny through the window. He was already crying, his mandible jittering, his eyes leaking tears. Before Jack drove away, Randy said two words that Danny couldn't hear but could see: *Help me.*

Then they were gone, and only the abomination remained. Across Hilman Street, between a row of old metal garbage cans and a dilapidated house, Grandma Crowley was standing—no, that wasn't right—*levitating* above a sewer grate, her feet bent and contorted, a black silhouette against a stark white sky. Slowly, she raised a finger to her lips. *"Shhhhh."*

Danny found himself unable to move.

"Shouldn't have removed it," she told him, removing a maggot from her face. Her voice sounded virile. "Did you know that even insects are sentient beings, Danny? But they mean nothing. The black goat is coming from the dark recesses of the cosmos, and you cannot stop him. God cannot stop him. No one can. It's inevitable, and you are doomed to the expanse that makes hell look like paradise."

Her dark, contrasting figure faded until it disappeared.

Danny now stood alone on the curb, frozen from shock and from cold. Steam effused from his mouth with repeated breaths. He decided to go home and wait to hear from Randy, if he ever did again.

Prior to turning and taking off, Danny glanced back at the Cadillac. It sat rumbling idly at the STOP sign at the most dangerous intersection of town, its exhaust spuming smoke. Before it pulled out onto the road, Danny noticed something incredible.

Randy was looking out through the back windshield, eyes fixed on the spot where Ethel had been floating moments ago.

Randy had seen her there, too.

Someone had finally seen her, too.

Chapter Ten

While Danny and Randy parted ways, Amy looked under Danny's bed for the anti-anxiety medication. She tore his room apart looking for them and couldn't find squat. She wiped at tears now and again, padded out of his room, and ransacked the house in search for the medication. It didn't turn up anywhere; she even went as far as rummaging through the garbage, both inside and out. That meant either Danny had taken them, or they'd simply disappeared.

Her son needed her; she knew she had to let go of her adulting mind and focus, believe in the unreal again and accept the fact that the unknown existed. When she passed through the living room, she stopped, feeling overwhelmed and trapped. Outside looked like Christmastime with all the snow. An unnerving silence filled the room, the entire house, maybe all of Tinney Lane. She concentrated on the memory of her dearly-departed mother and closed her eyes, closing out the world of reality she knew so well, like so many others did.

"Mom. Ethel, are you here with me? Are you terrorizing my son? Answer me, if you are. So help me, if you are behind this, I will figure out what's going on and put a stop to it. Mark my words, woman, you hurt my son, I'll dig up your body and destroy what's left."

She felt a momentary relapse of self after vocalizing these words, because she didn't want to mean any of them. She, unlike David, had always gotten along well with her mother. They had both grown together, mother and daughter, through several decades and sundry experiences.

Slowly, she opened her eyes and looked around the room. The throw pillows sat plumply on the couch. The chair remained motionless. The coffee table, stacked with magazines, reflected falling snow—the only apparent movement. Any sign of ghostly phenomena failed to comply to her command. Nothing. And it made her all the more dismayed and disappointed for her son and his well-being.

"You old, dead coward!"

A shrill noise from the kitchen made her jump. Her insides seemed to jump, too, as if her spirit, for a nanosecond, had left her body through her head before falling back in place.

Hand clutching chest, she had no memory of whirling around to the shrieking phone.

That's all it was. Ringing. Ringing. Ringing.

Her heart pounded in her tightened chest as her feet carried her to the noise. The closer she got to the Motorola, the faster it throbbed like kick drums in her ears. She dreaded who hung on the other line, but picked it up, turned it on, and put it against her ear anyway.

"Hello?" Her voice sounded pathetically weak, so she said, "Who is this?"

This you, Mom, calling from the grave in Lancing Cemetery? To tell me my son's joined you there and that you have dominion over his disembodied spirit?

Pum-pum-pum—blood surging through the hot arteries in her neck. Her face was on fire.

"Answer me!" she nearly yelled.

"Mrs. Willow?"

Oh my God, the police are calling to tell me the worst... Danny has died. They found his body—

"Mrs. Willow, this is Principal Redding. I am calling to inform you that Danny will not be attending Ducougery High any longer after his outburst here in my office earlier today."

"You mean he's not in school?"

"Not as of about two today. He'll have to find some other educational—"

"He left school at two?"

"That's right!" He was almost yelling at her. "He and his

friend, that... Randy Wayde boy, left together nearly an hour ago."

A single tear rolled down her check as this biblical information rushed through her, and the only thought that entered—invaded her mind, was: *where is he now?*

Oh God, where is my boy now?

"Mrs. Willow! Are you listening to me?" He was screaming in her ear.

She focused on her descending tear, one of a million more a real mother would spill while worrying over her beloved child.

She hung up the phone—slammed it down with such force, it broke, and cursed the principal, using every foul word her distraught mind could conjure up. When she was done cursing him, she cursed herself. The Motorola was the only usable phone in the house. They'd gotten rid of the landline last month; it was a worthless commodity compared to the cell phones they used much, much more. Home phones? What were those? Who used those dinosaur communication devices these days?

The kitchen was dark and gloomy. The stove was cool, of course, but she suddenly saw herself slaving over a hot one, cooking food that her baby boy would never eat again. She imagined his body starving, cold and empty, his mind neither learning nor expanding. *He could be dead.*

She ran out the door without her shoes on, and without any memory of grabbing the keys off the fob in the hallway. The keys were just there, abracadabra. The car seemed to start up automatically, but the garage door opened way too slow for her liking. She backed the SUV out of the garage before it had a chance to fully open and scraped some paint off the roof of the vehicle.

Who cares? A car is a replaceable object.

But a human, Danny Willow, in particular, was a sacred, precious living soul she could never replace.

Whether he's dead or alive, I'm going to find my baby.

Chapter Eleven

As fate, coincidence, or just dumb luck would have it, Danny returned home just minutes—single digit numbers, after his mother drove down Tinney Lane in her SUV. In fact, he could smell the choking stink of exhaust fumes as he ran up the walkway to the front door, with no knowledge that it had come from her vehicle.

"Mom!" he hollered, slamming the door shut behind him. "Mom, are you home? I need to talk to you!"

He marched down the hallway and into the kitchen. The clock read: 3:12. Danny immediately noticed something out of place lying on the island amid the scarce light of day: mom's broken Motorola.

Broken phone? No Randy. Just days remaining!

Danny took a seat on the couch and grabbed a pillow. It was square and frilly and made of durable suede. It had come with the couch, which his parents had bought with their income tax returns years ago. Gripping it, he gazed at the fireplace, into the black, rectangular firebox, where logs had fueled fires every single winter for fourteen short years. As his mind reeled, he pulled his hands in opposite directions. The pillow held up, but he kept pulling, squeezing, grimacing, gazing, hating, fearing, burning. This pillow, he imagined—he believed—was Grandma Crowley's head, and he was attempting to tear it apart. He cursed her name in his mind. The firebox stared back at him, Stygian black—the way he'd been feeling since all this began. He remembered standing over her as she lay in the casket, and of how he felt about her *before* she'd spoken, before her face had ripped apart and sprouted a buffet of insects. That was a clue, was it not? The resentment, the hate... the emptiness was not a byproduct of this madness, it was a precursor.

What happened? What happened before the funeral? Before

her death? Before she got old and feeble? What did she do to me in my much younger days?

What, indeed?

"I haaate you!" he screamed. He'd managed to find some inner strength, because the tension in the pillow broke, and fluffy white stuffing came spilling out. It fell onto the coffee table, then onto the floor, and lastly onto his shoes, and it all reminded him of Ethel's frizzy white hair. "Do you know that?"

He got up and screamed, lamented to the dark powers that be, "If you're gonna take me, do it. Don't wait. Do it now, or not at all!" He started crying again. "Do it now." He wept into his hands. "Why? What did I do to you? Whatever you're gonna do, tell me before this is all over. I want to know. I have to know."

After he let out some of his pent-up emotions, he stormed out of the room, but stopped when he heard an object fall onto the living room carpet.

Upon turning around, he discovered what it was: one of the many framed photographs which sat over the fireplace mantle. Now it lay face-down on the floor. Danny went over and picked it up. It was the picture they'd taken on Tappan Lake during the summer of 2016. Five of them were huddled together in the cramped photo: Danny, mom, dad, Lanny and Grandma, arms wrapped around shoulders, the lake still and the sun shining down behind them. Everyone was happy and smiling.

"What are you trying to show me?"

Snap! The glass frame cracked right over Danny's face in the picture. This minute crack, which looked more like a scuff, or scratch, deepened. Then it ran right, across dad's face, then farther right, across mom's. This single offset crack evolved into others that ran every which way across the picture of his whole family.

Everybody's face except Lanny's and Ethel's. By the time Ethel ended this elaborate magic trick from the grave, half the glass cover was in tact while the other half had been reduced to sparkling powder.

Danny threw the picture, frame, glass and all, into the fireplace. "I see. So it's not just me you want. You want my dad and my mother too. Well, you're not gonna get them. Do you hear me? Hello?"

Although she didn't answer, not verbally, anyway, she did in her own insidious manner.

The photograph—and nothing else—burst into flames. Only Lanny and Ethel were spared from the hungry flames. Danny, David, and Amy burned, warped, and melted into oblivion.

Chapter Twelve

The Waydes lived out on Larson Ridge, the closest thing to the countryside, save Piker's Hill, in the span of three counties. Their residence, a dilapidated single-wide, stood on three acres deep in a valley surrounded by hills, brooks, and elderly trees with some of the most twisted boughs. Dad drove erratically along a winding road, and Randy sat in the backseat, afraid for his life. Dad screamed at him, told him how bad he was going to get it today, just like he did every time prior to beating him. The stench of alcohol reeked in the Cadillac, which almost veered off the road half a dozen times. Randy cried and wailed, the thought of jumping out of the moving vehicle seemingly better than the thought of going home with this man.

"He needs my help," Randy said. "Danny needs my help, Dad."

"What you need is a good whippin', you no-good little loser. When we get home, you're going to see what punishment feels like in a nasty way, boy. Now, I don't wanna hear no more until we get there. Understand? Understand?"

"Yeah." He thought about Danny, about the apparition he'd seen, and about Grandma Crowley, whose blackened figure had been floating a foot above the ground like a hanging Halloween prop.

What else can she do?

Randy glared hostilely at his dad in the rear-view mirror. He resented the man with the same poisonous passion he imagined Danny felt for his grandmother. Both were monsters wrapped in human bodies. But they all had to have a weakness, didn't they? A chink somewhere in their armor?

Randy knew his dad's: alcohol. It served as his fuel as well, a powerful stimulant that had a tendency to dismantle his head, along with his motor functions. That's what was happening now, on this snow-covered winding road. The alcohol made him swerve all over the place. The man didn't even have enough common sense to flick on the wipers to combat the falling flakes.

The Cadillac swiped an oak on the right side of the road. Dad belted out the eff word and spun the wheel left. A tire dove into a chuckhole; the vehicle bounced wildly. Randy's head collided with the roof. Dad tried righting. This time the car hit Mr. Himer's wooden fence, breaking it and scaring some horses on the property. A log pinned the car to the spot. Dad leaned over the wheel and ralphed. *This is my time to get away. Danny needs me, and I need him.*

Randy got out of the car, which began to smoke from the hood. He ran east, the way they'd traveled, with one destination in mind: Ducougery Library. Surely he could start by finding some information there.

He looked back once while he ran. Thick, dense smoke had engulfed the car. Dad still hadn't gotten out, but Randy could hear him cursing. And Randy didn't use Pockter's Ridge Road to get back to town; he took a shortcut through the woods, which should get him there in just two miles instead of five.

He assured himself that nothing could stop these legs, not Dad, not Ethel, not Lucifer, not anybody.

And nothing did.

***

He made it to Ducougery Library less than twenty minutes later. It crowded the corner of Solman Street like a big, overgrown stone weed. It somehow looked out of place in its current location, surrounded by dinky local businesses that he and Danny frequented. But never, in the sixteen years he'd been alive, could he remember sprinting to a library, of all places, so willingly, so excited to study. But here he was, and that's how he felt.

He was sweating and panting when he threw the entrance door

open and entered the building. A small bell rang overhead. Two librarians standing behind a desk turned around immediately, startled. Randy said, "Sorry. Didn't mean to barge in here. Can I use your computer?"

One librarian, a big-eyed, blue-haired old woman in a blue dress, pointed with a stamper in her hand.

Randy stormed past several rows of books, from a to z, the scent of old paper strong. Aside from himself and the two librarians, the place was empty.

He found the rank of computers at the back, past the bathrooms and children's section. Randy parked his butt in the first chair. He moved the mouse and brought the screen to life. Blue light illuminated his face as he began to type.

What is the black goat of a thousand young?

He pressed enter and waited, and boom, something came up. The top of the page read, *Demonic Entities,* so he clicked on that. The text that appeared was small, so he got closer to the screen. He narrowed his eyes as he read the red font against a black background.

The black goat of a thousand young is a malevolent diety from Sumerian folklore. It's true name is Litius. It controls a 1000 legions of dead souls, and is one of the gatekeepers, as well as reigning demons, of hell. It's featured in several different religions, from Catholicism to Christianity to Islam to Judaism. The demon can be controlled by using either alchemy or witchcraft, granting wishes of all kinds, from wealth and power to love and prosperity. It's been written that this entity is one of few who can even grant immortality. But, according to texts, one must sacrifice a specific number of children in special rituals involving bloodletting and torment. If any part of the spell is befouled, Litius can keep and punish the conjurer's soul for eternity. There are, however, supposed ways around this, such as reciting special passages of text from certain grimoires, which can supposedly redirect the demons' powers back to the spellcaster. But these must be spoken in full earnest and with perfect respect. Some believe Litius lives in places of deep shadow where life does not grow; others believe that Litius lives in one of the star constellations of the Zodiac, and can sometimes return to earth on rare celestial events when a grand witch has accepted her fate in the form of Dark Death. However, this takes decades of careful planning, devotion, and will only work if a grand witch has secured a host in which to entrap the demon. The demon can become mortal from that point on, and control the world under the conjurer's own devising. If this happens, the host's soul loses its Godlife and ceases to exist. It can never be redeemed or brought back.

The power a conjurer must possess to do any of this is astronomical, as it goes beyond simple incantation. It involves fasting during certain days and nights of the year, frequent blood drinking of the host, the slaughter and torment of hundreds of young who haven't yet reached adolescence, in addition to perfecting the concoction of a special potion that's been said to be able to render one invisible.

The final rite needed in order to complete the conjuration is simply a mark, or brand from the grand witch. This facilitates the connection between the host, the witch, and Litius, granting the latter two access into the world, on Samhain.

According to Jonathan Nebell, a historian of folklore and the occult, no incantation can work if the host doesn't provide the conjurer a *link* into the world. As of now, no one knows exactly what this *link* is or how it's established, but many have speculated on what it could be. These theories range from complex curses to the desecration of souls through theft of the Akashic Records.

Randy leaned back, his eyes widened in puzzled shock. At the bottom of the screen, there was an artist's rendition of what the black goat of 1000 young looked like. And it wasn't pretty.

This was most of the information he needed, not all, but enough to get a good idea of what was going on. He had to get in touch with Danny quickly, before all this ensued, and tell him that he was essentially a host to a demon that could eradicate all the light in the known universe.

Chapter Thirteen

Danny hadn't been to Ethel and Lanny Crowley's house in nearly three years. The Willows used to visit every Sunday, had lunch or dinner, shot the breeze, played board games, laughed, and watched TV. This was before Ethel had taken ill. It seemed that her onslaught of health issues happened all of a sudden, too, not there one day, then crippling her the next. Thinking back on this, Danny realized something he hadn't taken into consideration until just now. There had been days—a lot of days—when he went home from Ethel's, feeling cold, clammy, tired and weak. This didn't happen every Sunday, of course, but often enough to make him furrow his brows at the thought. *Was she doing something to me then, all that time, all those years, using me in some corrupt way?*

That's what he was determined to find out.

He stood alongside Ray Lane, a country road, snow falling all around him, looking at the house where Ethel once lived and Lanny now owned. *Did he know what she was?* Danny thought. *Was he in on it too, or was he just a fool who had no clue?* Lanny wasn't a stupid man, but Danny had never considered him the sharpest tool in the shed, either. As Randy used to say: *He creeps me out.*

And it took quite a lot to creep Randy out.

Danny wished he was here now, standing beside him on Ray Land, looking across a one-acre yard to a quaint Colonial by woods, as a reinforcement. But he wasn't. Randy was probably getting it in the mouth again, and Danny was alone on this journey.

He took a deep breath in and let it out, the cold whirring around him in a cold cyclone. Then he marched forward, toward the Crowley house. He walked with purpose, with pizzazz, the snow falling all around him. It had frozen on the grass, stiffening the millions of blades, making them sparkle.

Lanny's Lincoln was not parked in the driveway, so that was a plus. He could've been off in half a dozen places: grocery shopping, getting his junk-mobile fixed, playing poker with his buddies, working his odd jobs, anything.

Danny didn't pay him much thought. He walked, his feet crunching over frozen, spiked grass. No vehicles had passed on the road behind him, so when one finally did, he started running. With his rotten luck, it was probably Lanny coming back. Danny didn't want Lanny to find him nosing around the property.

He hid behind some bushes that separated the vast yard from the narrow driveway. There, he watched and waited. And listened. It *clanked* loudly, sounding similar to the lemon Lanny had been driving for a good ten years.

But when it came into view, Danny realized it wasn't Lanny's Lincoln after all. It was a van instead. A long trail of black exhaust followed it. Poor automobile looked liable to break down right then and there on the highway.

It didn't.

It passed, leaving behind an almost perfectly perpendicular line of toxic smoke Danny could smell.

He continued, quickening his pace. He approached the house, an old-fashioned two-story Colonial with a gabled roof, black shutters, and a jutting, off-centered chimney that looked older than dinosaur bones. There was a patio on the side where Lanny liked to sit and drink beer and read newspapers and have get-togethers. On the other side was a car port cluttered with broken lawnmowers and yard tools. Danny stared at the upper windows— the ones to Ethel's room—as he approached, making his way to the snow-dusted turnaround. *Is she up there at this moment, looking back? Waiting for me? Smiling? Is she with me at all right now?*

He felt watched, although acute paranoia could make just about anyone feel that way, too.

He ignored his fears and climbed the five steps leading up to the front door. There was no porch, just a stoop and a small roof held up by two posts. *Lanny could be inside, couldn't he? His car could be in the shop, somebody could've borrowed it—*

He tried the door, forcing these anxious thoughts back the best he could. Locked. Of course it was. If it wasn't going to budge, he'd just try the windows. But after doing so, he found that they weren't opening either. *It's secure. I don't have a way inside.*

The cacophony of yet another motor captured Danny's attention. This time it sounded big and heavy, like the roar of a diesel engine. Not so concerned, Danny turned and watched as an eighteen-wheeler *whooshed* past a grove of oaks on the opposite side of the road, knocking down snow from several boughs. *Nope, not Lanny.*

It didn't occur to Danny, not really, not until now, anyway, that Lanny's nearest neighbor could be home next door, watching him. The bungalow on the right had no lights burning in its windows, and although there were no vehicles in the driveway, there could have been one in the small garage on the side.

I can't worry about it. If they're there, they're there; this is something I'm going to have to risk.

Feeling strapped for time, Danny circumvented the house. He skulked along the left side of it, past the carport and to the back, where a well stood by the entrance to the woods. Time and weather had cracked and crumbled most of the stones; some were falling in, and if you got too close, the stench of foul water at the bottom roiled your gut. It was making Danny sick now. Copper mines used to run underground along this land, Lanny had once told him, but whether Lanny had been telling the truth was another issue. That indifferent *stare* of his... made Danny wonder. Really wonder.

Danny couldn't take any chances; he had to assume that his uncle was a toady for his grandmother, because if he was, he could be just as dangerous, if not more so. Lanny was made out of flesh and blood. Grandma was not.

Not yet, anyway.

The reek of old copper grew stronger as Danny breezed by the well. Snowy leaves and deadfall crowded the entryway to the woods like a barrier. He used to explore these woods with Lanny, back during another time, it seemed, when Lanny used to call him Danny and Ethel wasn't a monster.

Danny tried the back door, expecting resistance—and that's what he got. The house was locked up tight. He tried pushing up the window that opened into the kitchen. It told him no, too. He had no way in, not in this rural fortress.

At least not without shattering glass or prying a door open with a tool from the carport. That's what he'd look for, a crowbar, a hammer, anything capable of breaking a mundane lock. A window would be easier, he thought, although messier.

Any way I can.

I'm getting inside this house if it's the last thing I do.

Suddenly, he felt watched.

Danny whirled around. The woods were quiet, white, desolate. There was no movement, no wavering of branches, not even a hiss of wind.

Grandma Crowley?

Lanny?

He hadn't heard the sound of any motors, and Uncle Lanny's clunker would've been audible to someone with bad hearing.

"Grandma? Ethel?"

He panned the small, sloping backyard. Everything remained still.

I'm stalling.

Danny jogged back around to the carport. Inside, it was slightly warmer but still far too cold for October. The county usually never got this much snow, not even in the winter months. It made him ponder the topic of photosynthesis and wonder if, he was, in fact, Ethel Crowley's own form of fuel, or energy. Perhaps she was drawing all her power from him from some hellish netherworld. Who knew?

These sudden thoughts were like an epiphany. They made a lot of sense.

Danny was Ethel's sunlight, the nutrients she needed in order to grow. And so far, it seemed like she was flourishing.

What will happen when she's finished?

He wanted that question answered more than any other, even though he knew it involved hearing an answer he didn't think he could take.

Thoughts ran through his mind like a spinning carnival ride as he searched for a hammer, a crowbar, anything Lanny's carport had to offer. But he didn't find many tools; a rusted hacksaw, screwdrivers, pliers. It took him a little digging, but he eventually found a tire iron. Danny picked it up. It felt nice and heavy in his hands, his skewed version of a house key.

Relieved, he turned and ran into what felt like a brick wall covered in plaid. At first he thought it was Grandma, coming to claim him. But it wasn't. He knew this person's breath, and thought: Lanny. *He's gotten his car fixed, now it runs smooth, and he coasted up the driveway to find me, this burglar, going through stuff in his carport.* But that was wrong, too.

"Whoa, whoa! It's just me—Randy!"

Danny had cocked the tire iron back, over his head, ready to flatten the skull of something evil.

His shock turned to surprise, and his surprise turned to realization. Randy jumped out of the way.

"Sorry, man," Randy said, eyes as wide as a frightened animal's. "I didn't mean to scare you."

"Well, you did. How in the world did you get here?"

Randy smiled slyly. "My dad wrecked on the way home. I got out and cut through the woods. I'm just glad my crappy sense of direction actually worked well." He laughed. Danny forced a smile. "I'm here for you, like I said I'd be, and no drunken idiot is going to stop me. I'm not going home again, man. I've got to move on. I know we're not supposed to run away from what haunts us, but some things don't go away and can't be beaten. Am I supposed to dish out his crap every day? Are you supposed to let Grandma Crowley use your body?"

Danny arched his eyebrows. "What?"

"You don't know, that's right. I went to the library." He laughed again. "Me, the library. I got on their computer and researched the black goat of a thousand young. It's some kind of demon."

"Is that it? What else did you read?" Danny's curiosity skyrocketed.

"That it takes special rituals to summon it. Rituals that take years, decades. It all points to witchcraft, wizardry. I think your grandma was a witch."

"A witch?"

"I think so."

Danny let this sink in. It was like trying to digest a whole Thanksgiving dinner in a matter of seconds. Could it be that she'd dabbled in witchcraft and the occult during her breathing, heart-beating days? It made sense. A lot of it. Now, if they could just break into the house, they could perhaps find some evidence to validate this theory.

"He's not home, is he?" Randy asked, looking at the tire iron in Danny's hands.

"No, I don't think so, but I want to get in and out fast. If he is gone for some extended length in time, who knows whether Ethel will alert him somehow."

Randy furrowed his brows. "What? You think he might be in on it too?"

Danny was cold, but his face felt hot. "Don't know for sure, but I just feel that he is. He took care of her forever. He's had to known something."

"And you know I feel about him. Gives me the creeps." Randy

shook. "Are you going to use that as a battering ram or something?" He nodded to the tire iron. "Or to club me over the head with?"

Danny chuckled uncomfortably. "How else do we get in? All the doors and windows are sealed shut."

Randy clapped him on the shoulder and reassured him with a warm smile. "Did you forget who you're talking to?"

Danny smiled brightly.

***

Randy used a paperclip and a Swiss army knife to pick the lock on the back door. It took him a matter of seconds.

"Easy peasy," Randy said to Danny. "No mess, and Lanny will never know either of us were here."

"Let's hope."

"Yeah, let's hope your grandmother isn't here right now watching us.

"How did you know how to—"

"Remember when Marina's got robbed?"

"You did that?" Danny said flatly.

"Not exactly, but you could say I was an accessory. I learned it from Henry Lallon, you remember?"

"The kid who got sent to, like, adult prison before his junior year in high school?"

"That's him. He was trouble with a capital T. If I hadn't been held back, I might have ended up with him, probably. I wouldn't have ever met you, I don't think. You're a good influence on me, you know? Before today, my dad even said so."

Danny smiled and felt his heart burn bright.

Randy opened the back door for him. "After you."

Danny entered. Randy followed him inside and shut the door behind him.

They were standing in an immaculate kitchen that looked clean enough to resist germs. It smelled nice, too, redolent with the aroma of bleach. *The kitchen of someone who makes sure no fingerprints are left behind...*

Wait a sec...

Lanny had always had a habit of keeping the house clean, inside and out, despite his tendency for hoarding. Danny remembered him washing dishes immediately after every dinner they used to have, and always cleaning the siding every other week or so. But Lanny's neat-freak nature languished when it came to his own personal hygiene. His breath was usually foul, the odor barely masked by a piece of Wrigley's Doublemint, and his skin was often broken out and oily. These two incongruous details stood out like a sore thumb to Danny, two more files of evidence to store along with everything else.

They passed by a broom closet, between a sink and dinner table, a fridge and stove, and snaked their way through the cramped hallway, past a bathroom and into a spacious living room. The carpet was spotless, royal blue. A window overlooked the front yard over the plush sofa, and Danny watched the snow fall and fall. Any sign of green grass had been covered by the glorious white stuff. He turned back to Randy, who looked around the room. There was a TV in the corner; a recliner in the opposite one, where a bookcase filled with crime novels was set. Behind the bookcase was the flight of stairs that led up to Ethel's room.

Randy picked up a photograph off the fireplace mantel. Danny looked at it and said, "Doesn't look like a witch, does she?"

"No, but looks can be deceiving."

"We're not sure she's a witch yet, anyways, are we?"

"Pretty sure, but not ab positive."

Danny didn't crack a smile.

"Some levity humor there, Dan."

"Please don't call me Dan. Feels weird. That's what Lanny calls me."

"Not Danny? That is weird. Maybe he just calls you that now

since you're older."

"Maybe. Come on, her room's this way."

"I saw a movie once. Can't remember the name, but this coven of witches had all these trap doors hidden throughout their monastery—"

"Lanny, a carpenter?" Danny laughed. Now, that was funny. It wasn't that the guy was necessarily bad with his hands; it was that Danny had never seen him fix or build anything. He vocalized this point. "I saw him pick up a hammer once. Held it like a girl. Swung it like a girl. And missed the nail, which had a big head. My mom did better on her first try."

"Could be putting on a fake front, in case she or anyone ever caught on."

Danny considered this. Putting on a fake front for that long, however, seemed a stretch. But look how far Ethel had already come. Past the brink of death. Back from death itself. Speaking and walking and levitating and turning into obscenities he wished were a thing of nightmares. She'd defied the laws of physics, so couldn't Lanny have kept a secret all his life?

Danny didn't doubt it anymore; he just wasn't sure now. *Anything's possible.*

Danny led him to the bottom of a long, dark, narrow staircase. The steps went straight up to a door at the top. There were no windows here, no landing, no hallway, no additional rooms. Even in the daylight you could barely make out the last few steps. It seemed like a bridge to some alternate world, one steeped in dark mystery and bleak atmosphere.

Danny climbed, Randy followed. They creaked up what felt like a thousand stairs. Each groan or moan of floorboard sounded like the dying bellow of an animal. It was too dark for daylight to cast shadows of either boy on either the wall or the slanted ceiling, which they had to hunch down in in order to get to the door.

Danny opened it, and they entered. He hadn't been in here in about five years, and couldn't remember what it looked like. The bed by the door was bare, the sheets nowhere, the mattress covered in stains. There were a million scratches on it, clawed all to hell by perhaps some feline from hell. A few springs jutted up from shredded, frayed fabric. Batting clung to the sharp ends of the springs like innards to spikes. Everything reeked. It reeked of a lot of things, a plethora of stinks ranging from foul to natural to unusual. There were so many, it was hard to discern one from the other.

Randy coughed. "What is that? Stinks."

"I have as little idea as you do. Let's search and find what we can. I don't want to be long."

"Just anything out of the ordinary?"

"Absolutely. And if you can help it, try not to make too big of a mess."

"Don't know how well I'll fare with that, but I'll try. Ransacking cleanly are two words that don't go together."

They went to work.

Danny first went to a cloth-covered table that was standing under a window which overlooked the front yard, the driveway, the road, and groves of trees. He checked under the table. He flipped four chairs over. He found a drawer in the table, but the drawer was empty. When he turned, he bumped the table and almost knocked it over. Even though it didn't fall, the cloth floated down off it and landed on the floor.

"Randy, look at this."

Randy got up, came over. "I saw that! On the computer at the library."

"Are you serious?"

"Yeah, it was all over the screen. Said that was the mark of the black goat of a thousand young."

Danny looked at the flat surface of the rounded table. The symbol wasn't carved into the wood; it had been scorched into it by heat or flame. Looked like it was a cohesive part of the table, itself, done by a careful hand. Couldn't have been done by Ethel, not the feeble one in the span of ten years before her death. And then there was Lanny, who couldn't hold a hammer—

Unless he could and didn't want anybody—even mom—to know.

They went back to work, rummaging, pulling stuff out of dark places, searching for vital information that could evidently shed light on the matter. The mess they were making grew by the second, becoming a Hoarder's episode that would take them awhile to clean up. As they ransacked the room, however, Danny became aware that he felt like an addict looking for drugs. Instead of hindering and hurting, this prescription would heal and cure. Randy was making lots of noise behind him, moving stuff, flipping through papers, pulling and pushing objccts, opening the closet door.

"Find anything?" Danny asked sometime during their raid on Grandma Crowley's empty house.

Empty. Let's hope it stays that way for awhile.

They both found things, but neither thoroughly inspected their findings until they had enough stuff to lump together. When they did, they sat beside each other on what remained of the bed—quite possibly the exact spot where Ethel had died days before—and gathered what mostly consisted of papers and photographs.

The first photograph showed Ethel at a young age—teens, twenties—sitting at a table that looked identical to the one Danny had found the symbols on. There were three other people sitting around it. Their hands were all linked together, and there were crystals and candles standing on the table. Though in monochrome, this picture actually reproduced color where the crystals lay. It reminded Danny of an old parlor trick, perhaps a séance popular in the 1800s... but this one was real—he could feel it. He could sense it. And he had all the proof he needed to make him know that.

Ethel's eyes were rolled back, with only the scleras showing, her hair floating about her head. Her brows were creased like twisted leather. She looked pretty but oh so creepy.

That was not all. The other three people at this séance were sitting there with their jaws dropped and their eyes agape as they watched the white, amorphic mass protruding from Ethel's mouth. It looked vaporous, though was thicker, and didn't resemble cotton at all. Upon closer inspection, Danny noticed faces in it—faces overlapping faces, some seemingly crying out, some smiling, some shouting mad.

"Ectoplasm!" Randy said this as if he'd seen it somewhere before.

"What's that?" Danny had heard of it before, but had no idea what it really was.

"Supposedly ghost matter, the physical manifestation of the dead through a medium. It's been debunked on a ton of those ghost shows I've seen. Dead souls channeling through her, I guess. I will say this, though—all the pictures they show on TV don't look nothing like that. It looks like cotton or cigarette smoke on TV. This picture... this gives me the heebie-jeebies."

"Me too."

Danny heard the next sound as clear as day: the thud of a car door. It came from outside, not far under the only window of Ethel's bedroom.

"Uh-oh," he muttered. "He's here. Lanny's here. We gotta put all this stuff ba—"

Randy stopped him. "We won't have time, man. Let's just split. We have to get outta here."

Danny's eyes flitted about the room. Randy helped him up. They went to the door, but Danny hesitated when he grabbed the knob. "Wait. Wait! We can't go this way."

"Why not?" Randy's voice was cracking, breaking.

"The front door! To get to the back, we have to go around. As soon as we make it down the stairs, he'll see us when he comes in. We got no way out of here."

"Sure we do." Randy rushed to the only window of the room

and unlocked it. Then he grabbed the handle. Danny watched him, one hand on the doorknob, the other holding the photograph. The look on Randy's face, however, told him that they had nothing to fear. The anxiety in his eyes had turned to glee, and his mouth supported a relieved smile.

"What do you see?" Danny heard himself nearly stutter.

"It's good, it's all good. We're in the clear. Some old fart in a Chevy Nova."

Danny felt his nerves lax. He let go of his grip on the door knob. His butt collided with and sunk into Ethel's bed. "Mr. Paulson. Lanny's next door neighbor."

Randy sat back down beside him. A mountain of evidence lay on the smelly, torn mattress between them.

They looked through the photographs first. There were several more of Ethel performing her preternatural tricks, some where the ectoplasm was just beginning to form, and others where it took definitive shape. In the early stages, the onlookers looked merely excited and eager. But the latter stages showed a much scarier story: one guy missing from the toppled chair he'd been sitting in... a woman shrieking... At full capacity, Ethel's mouth was open much farther than naturally possible, and the grotesque number of faces were a boggle to the mind. One didn't look human. At all. Danny couldn't begin to describe it, and didn't think he'd ever want to.

After they looked through these, they flipped through some others. One depicted Ethel holding Danny's mother. Amy lay in her arms, wrapped in a pink blanket, smiling for the camera. Something about the photo didn't sit right with Danny. It didn't have to do with the creepy expression on his grandmother's face or the fact that she was holding his mom. The... *timeline* was askew somehow, someway, but Danny ignored this and flipped through photo after photo.

"Here. What's this symbol?" Danny asked Randy. A twisted doodle was drawn in what looked like blood on a concrete wall.

Randy shrugged. "You got me. Maybe some Pagan symbol. I don't know for sure." He furrowed his brows. "Where is that? Any idea where it was taken?"

"Underground? Looks like a sewer. A cave or something."

"No, because, see?" Randy held up a larger picture—one of the same room, with a single concrete wall surrounded by four others covered with board panels. A subsequent picture revealed a wooden altar in the center of the room.

Still another photo showed a baby lying on the alter. Danny, who'd seen plenty of pictures of his mom throughout fourteen years, knew what she looked like as a baby. She had a sloping forehead, red tufts of wild hair, little black eyes, a slightly upturned nose. She lay there, on an altar, in an unfamiliar room.

Danny set the photograph down. When he picked up the next one, it practically jumped out of his hand. He let out a low shriek and recoiled as the picture landed face-down on the floor. Time slowed. His heart didn't resume beating until much later, it seemed.

When it did, Randy asked him, "What? What did you see?" He reached down for the picture.

"No! Don't!"

But Randy's hand was faster than Danny's plead. "What? I don't see nothing wrong with it."

Danny dared to take another look, bracing himself before he did. When his eyes met with the jolly smile of Ethel helping Amy learn to walk, he relaxed.

The best he could, anyway.

I did not see Ethel plunging a knife into my baby mother's chest while she screamed, blood jetting, gushing, Lanny laughing, Ethel grinning hatefully, while some... beast emerged from the darkness behind them all.

What had I seen?

Another trick? Another hallucination?

Danny turned to Randy. "When you saw her..."

"Your grandmother?"

"Yes, when you were driving away, what did she look like?"

"Floating, levitating, transparent."

"Transparent?" Danny found himself sounding doubtful. "You mean, see-through? You could see through her?"

"Yeah, why?" Randy looked puzzled.

Danny nodded. "How transparent was she?"

"Quite a bit. Why?"

Danny shook his head studiously. "That's why you didn't see her in the lunchroom when I got nailed with that ball. You weren't able to yet."

"What are you saying? I don't understand."

"After I told you everything, from beginning to end, you saw her. You saw her 'cause I helped you see her. I made you believe."

"Yeah, and 'cause I hate the woman's guts. Anyone who's trying to kill my best friend is a mortal enemy of mine."

"Yes, but still, I helped bring you to my level, don't you see? Every time I saw her, she was really there, only to me, because she somehow... sucked me in, I guess you could say."

"So you're saying that anyone can see her too?"

"Exactly! All they have to do is hear my story and believe."

"Okay..."

"When *I* saw her levitating there, she wasn't transparent to me. I saw her like I see you now. In a totally physical body."

"How can that be?"

Danny looked off into space. "I don't know."

Randy clapped him on the shoulder. "I think I might know, actually."

Danny was all ears. "What?"

"Just a theory, but you had only told me that story minutes before, seconds before. Maybe it was all so new to me..."

"That it takes time to cement?" Danny lifted a brow.

"Possible. Who knows?"

"I wish I knew."

"We're going to, man, we're going to figure this out. Let's keep sifting through this stuff."

Randy curiously flipped through a series of old, loose photographs. "Mundane, mundane, mundane, mundane, mundane, m—"

They suddenly fluttered out of his hands, all except one last remaining picture. His eyes fixed on it as it hypnotized him. His mouth also dropped open and a groan escaped. His hand began to shake. Danny leaned in. "What do you see?"

They both stared, transfixed. Dumbfounded. Lost. Catatonic. Terrified. No background noise within a hundred miles was loud enough to break them from this monumental sight. Not even the hottest supermodel could take such a mesmerizing picture. They stared for some time, unable to breathe or think.

It was another photo of the boarded basement with the altar. Except in this, the altar had blood on it, Ethel was kneeling on broken glass, crystals gripped in each hand, and the concrete wall before her was *open.* It wasn't open in the way a door would stand open, mounted into a frame and screwed into the foundation. The odd opening went *into* the wall, beyond the wall, past what humans believe is matter and substance. And what was coming out of that opening, that chunk of space, was some kind of monster. It held no resemblance to any gargoyle Danny had seen perched on church buildings or in a rubber suit in horror movies. Because this thing wasn't fictitious. No special make-up effects artist could construct something so horrifying, so fear-inducing. It had not one shape but many shapes, a hundred dark, arrogant faces. Forget horns, forget pitchforks—those were the stuff of legends. Its eyes were *forever,* bottomless. It didn't have teeth the way humans or animals did, nor did it walk or resemble the upright posture of man. It was a black entity from the deepest regions of hell, and Ethel had somehow, sometime, let this thing through. Danny and Randy were now witnesses to perhaps the first shred of proof of spiritual evil, captivating their undivided attention in all its malice and dark desire. And it gazed back at them, *through* them on this nearly century-old albumen silver print, as if it were seeing them here, now, today.

Danny had no recollection of what jarred him out of his daze. It'd be hours before he realized he'd shoved the photograph into his pants pocket. Randy was shaking a little and wiping slobber off his bottom lip.

The rest of the pictures turned out to be mundane, and they didn't find a whole lot more, but it was surely not the end of their search.

There were pieces of paper, long, narrow, stained and ripped from some ancient tome, replete with diagrams and symbols and weird numbers written on them. Circles encompassed around triangles, five-pointed stars, and language that looked nothing like either of them had ever seen. The pages didn't *exactly* feel like paper; they were thicker, harder, and quite smelly, and Danny got the impression that they were the remnants of some archaic spellbook. He could feel the power they presented. They produced a tingling sensation in his hands as he held them.

Then, a light bulb went on inside his head, and his thoughts reverted back to the photograph of Ethel holding Amy in her arms.

"Timeline doesn't match up."

"What?" Randy asked.

"Sorry, thinking out loud. Where's the—oh, here it is."

Danny picked up the photograph and wagged it in his hand. "Look how old my grandma is in this picture."

"Hmm. Looks more like a grandma holding her grandchild."

"Just what I thought."

Randy nodded. "And how old was she when she died?"

"A hundred and three."

"Wow. She looks about eighty nine here."

"My thoughts exactly! Which begs the question... had she lied about her age? Just how old was she when she croaked?"

"When was your mom born?"

"1968, I believe."

"Well, we can do what I did again."

"What's that?"

"Go to the library. Dig some more there."

Danny smiled. "What are we waiting for, then?"

They got up. Randy accidentally knocked almost everything off the bed. Danny sauntered to the window, smiling, brimming with curiosity and realization.

"I could have sworn I saw this before. Like, not long ago before," Randy said.

Danny stopped and turned. "What?"

"This board. The wooden panel in this picture of this basement."

"Can't remember where?"

"You know what? Yes, I do!" Randy got up and reached for the doorknob to the closet, and Danny moseyed to the window, getting a glimpse of snowland.

Must've got his car fixed....

Lanny must've gotten his muffler replaced.

His Lincoln pulled up right outside. The door opened, and Lanny got out, clad in jeans and a leather coat. He jogged to the house, seemingly in a hurry.

Danny's sense of reality did a tailspin. The ground felt like it'd dropped away, perhaps into some strange abyss of its own. For the second time in just minutes he forgot how to breath and process ration thought.

He's here, he's coming, and there's only one way out.

Alive, that is.

Where I'm standing. This very window.

"Here," Randy said enthusiastically. "This is where I saw that wood—"

Danny turned around, barely listening, standing on wobbly feet.

"What is it?" Randy asked him. "What's wrong?"

"Lanny's here."

The front door opened; the front door slammed closed. The pounding thud of footsteps sounded hectic and rising. Coming close, coming fast.

"What do we do?" Danny squealed.

Randy acted quickly. The first thing he did was shove the bed, all ten or fifteen pounds of it, against the door. There was a lock on the knob, so he engaged it, too. Lanny was starting to push and pound on it by then, trying to gain entry. He was muttering and cursing, although Danny couldn't make out any actual words.

Randy pulled up on the window. Didn't budge. "Danny, help me with this."

How do I function?

"Danny, come on!"

Thud! Bang! Crack! The lock was working, but the door not so much. Another few rams and he'd be past the first deterrent.

I'm not here. I'm not me. I'm a witness to this, nothing more.

I don't know what to do.

I don't know how to do it.

Who am I—

Though frozen, Danny gained his bearings when Randy gave him a good, hard smack across his cheek. Things came into focus and starting making sense again. Lanny, old Uncle Lanny was trying to break in and kill them, and Randy desperately needed his help to open the window so that they could escape.

"Snap out of it, man. We've gotta go!" Randy's voice sounded lucid and real.

Danny lent Randy his strength. Together, they pulled the window upward. It opened with a hissing screech. It had been painted over one too many times; the paint acted as a barrier. But they managed. And as they did, Lanny managed to break the lock. Now he was struggling against the bed. His face was fury red, moist with sweat. He didn't look like a loving relative anymore, but a trained killer bent on foiling their escape.

"Danny!" Randy's voice.

Danny turned back. The window was open all the way. "You go first. Hurry."

Danny looked back. Lanny kicked the door; the bed slid.

"Go, go, go!" Randy pushed Danny into motion.

Danny climbed through the opening, out onto the snow-covered roof. It was flat here, the frosty surface of shingles slippery under his feet. He looked back at Randy and offered a hand.

"No, no. Just go, I got this."

Randy was halfway out the window already, moving with fluid grace and catlike speed. Lanny shouted obscenities, and for a fleeting second, Danny wondered if he was an imposter, someone who just happened to look exactly like his uncle. The man he'd dined with hundreds of times, the guy who'd given him some of the best birthday and Christmas presents any kid could ever ask for, was yelling death threats at him and his friend. *Fourteen years of deceit. Fourteen years of putting on a front, just to trick somebody—how do—*

"Move it!" Randy bellowed. "He's almost in."

Danny took his steps lightly, making sure not to shift too much weight or drag his feet.

He grabbed the edges of the siding with his fingertips and walked sideways across the roof. Still flat here, all the way around to the rear. That was going to be a problem, wasn't it? They basically had to circumnavigate to get away, and by that time, Lanny could catch up, intercept them while they crept their way along. Then what? Play a rising game of catch me if you can? Hide and seek? How exactly were they going to get down? A fall could break their legs, injure a rib. Climbing down a pipe covered in snow? Ice?

For the moment, Danny listened and listened hard. Randy's breaths were hot and shallow in his left ear. Lanny's frantic shouts were louder, which meant he hadn't gotten into the room yet.

Then, he heard silence.

Randy's sudden yell made him slip. Danny regained his footing and looked back. Lanny was there at the window, reaching for Randy. Another inch or two and he would've had him. So Danny decided to shuffle his feet faster, settle his adrenaline down by thinking positive thoughts. *If Lanny comes out here, on this roof with us, his old, clunky body won't fare well, especially not with the frosted shingles.*

"Go, Danny, he's reaching."

Danny sped up some more. This part of the roof, of course, was the easy part. The hard part was coming right up, where the roof sloped downward before dropping off to a lower one and then to the pavement below. An uncalculated fall from that far, some twelve, thirteen feet, could be fatal.

Randy caught up, shuffling with him, seemingly a part of him, a siamese twin. They were both going as fast as they could without being reckless, making their way to where they'd have to let gravity do the rest.

There was one thing Danny heard that really bothered him. Disturbed him. Silence. That meant Lanny was somewhere back inside the house, likely rushing down the stairs, perhaps barreling through the living room and closing in on the back door.

"Wait," Randy told him. "Be real careful when you drop to the next roof below. When you hit that flat spot, shift all your weight back so that your momentum won't throw you off."

"Then what?"

Yeah, what do we do from there?

Randy's face failed to evince an answer.

Danny looked down. It was only a seven, eight-foot slide, but from this height and angle, it looked a mile long. The cold ground beneath the overhanging gutter intensified this effect. His heart burned in his throat. His legs quivered as he laid them out flat. He stalled, knowing he couldn't, knowing he shouldn't, and let his body go. He took his first butt-sled-ride down an inverted corner of a roof, gaining speed too quickly for his liking. He shifted his weight backward like Randy had advised, but found that it wasn't working. The icy shingles were just too slippery, so the laws of physics drove him onward, *downward,* across flat roofing and over the edge of the gutter. Before he fell out of the sky like a dead bird, he arched his waist and reached with clawed hands. His fingers caught hold of something, but it took him a second to realize what that was: the gutter. *Freezing.*

Saved by grace!

When he looked back up, he saw Randy flying toward him, going a hundred miles an hour, so it appeared, his crotch aimed toward his face.

If I weigh half of what Randy weighs, and I couldn't slow down, how in the world is he going to slow down?

And how is he not going to crash into me?

Aside from the slippery sound of Randy's speeding body coming toward him, Danny heard another noise that drove anxiety into him: footsteps. Boots across kitchen tile. Lanny was fast approaching, and that meant they had no chance. No chance whatsoever.

These thoughts held, but the gutter didn't. It broke under Danny's weight. It snapped from its place, and the soles of Randy's shoes collided with his face. Danny felt himself drop out of the sky, imagined Lanny standing beneath, arms open, prepared to catch him and carry him to Ethel's lair. Either that, or fall on his arm and dislocate it, maybe break both of his legs.

What Danny did was fall back-first onto the ground, right where grass almost ended and asphalt began. Then he opened his eyes and looked up. Randy hadn't tumbled off the roof. His lower half dangled over the hanging gutter while his upper half clung to the roof.

The footsteps had stopped. Danny felt a presence nearby, closer than Randy, and looked to the side. Lanny was standing right inside the kitchen, hands on hips, face obscured. Snow fell across his silhouette, and although Danny couldn't tell with certainty, he thought he was holding something in one of his hands.

A knife? That a knife?

A gun?

A metal pipe?

Danny sat up. *Time to take my medicine. Let's get this over with once and for all.*

Danny made his way to his feet, and his uncle stepped into the falling snow. "Danny Willow... what do you think you're doing breaking into my house, you and your friend here? Snooping around?"

Danny held up a hand. "Don't come near me!"

Lanny stepped forward. "You think you're smart going through your grandma's things, boy? Trying to figure it out? You don't know the half of it. This goes deeper than any of the photographs and your friend may have found upstairs. Does Ethel scare you?" He snickered humorlessly. "She scares me just as much, I assure you."

"What?" Danny took a step back, not wanting this man to get any closer.

"I'm not going to hurt you, Dan. This can all be settled easier if you just come inside. You alone. Keep your burglarizing friend out of this; it doesn't concern him."

"I believe it does," Danny said.

Lanny stared at him. "We both know it does not. And I'm not going to hurt him either, although I'd liked to be compensated for the broken things." Lanny's face went blank and flat. "Now come inside."

"Don't do it, man, don't listen to him!" Randy shouted.

Danny nodded. "He's right. You're with Ethel. You wouldn't have known to come here, knew where we were, if not for her."

"Well, you're right about that. I hoped things would be different once she was dead, but I'd been wrong, dead wrong." He evinced no amusement. "Inside. I'll explain everything."

Danny stepped back. In his peripheral vision, he could see Randy standing on the flat portion of the roof. He'd somehow made it to his feet.

"What do you got in your hand?" he shouted at his uncle.

"Inside, and I'll show you."

"No. Danny, he's trying to trick you!"

"Shut up!" Lanny whipped his head and looked up at Randy, meanwhile raising his hand just a little. In his grip wasn't a weapon, as Danny had thought, but one of those strange crystals he'd seen in Ethel's photographs.

"What is that?" Danny demanded.

"Inside, I tell." Lanny's voice was verging on rage.

"I.. gotta go home." Danny said.

Lanny smiled, and this time there was some humor in it. "You are home, Dan. Almost. The transitions won't be long now, and it won't hurt a bit."

"What is it, this transition? What does Ethel want with me?"

"Again, Danny, inside, and I will explain."

"Why can't you tell me out here?"

Lanny didn't reply, just stood there like a sadistic mannequin, and now, in Danny's peripheral vision, he could see the crystal shake violently in his hairy hand. Lanny was not only losing his patience but obviously what was keeping him sane. The air grew colder, as if signaling the coming of some errant storm. The snow fell harder, cutting its way diagonally through the frigid air. It didn't feel like fall, didn't feel like winter, but instead like some undiscovered season where savage beasts devoured light and warmth. Then Lanny's hand began to glow—the crystal in it was scintillating, releasing a strange energy that drew Danny's attention. *It's alive,* Danny thought. *That crystal in his hand is somehow alive.*

"Are you coming inside the easy way, Dan, or the hard way?"

But Danny backed away some more.

The crystal emanated a full range of colors, some so vivid they looked grab-able.

"Neither!" Randy shouted at him. "Don't do it, Danny. Don't listen to him; I knew he was wrong since the first time I met him."

Lanny's patience was dwindling. His eyes were colder than the air, his demeanor was worsening, and he seemed to inch closer without moving at all.

Danny backed away, closer to the neighbor's shed. Lanny stood perfectly still.

Then he wasn't.

He broke into a run, a bull-like sprint toward Danny, the glimmering crystal in his hand a disco ball of colors. It pierced the dim, bleak landscape, tarnishing it with an evil, mysterious energy. When snow fell onto the crystal, it turned the snow black.

Danny tried to run, and he started to... until he slipped on ice and found himself tumbling toward the ground. The fall hurt more here than the one from the roof. Lanny closed the distance quickly for his age and managed to trudge through snow without losing his footing once. But Randy intervened, leaping off the roof like a wrestler jumping off the ropes and catching Lanny during his descent. Both boy and man fell into thickening snow. Lanny landed safely while Randy landed head-first into the stone well. His body stiffened up before it came to rest on top of Lanny. His arms crisscrossed; his feet straightened and shook; his eyes rolled. He looked like he was having a seizure. Lanny struggled to get up, but Randy's body kept him parked on several inches of snow.

He's dead, Danny thought, *Randy's gotta be dead, and if he's not, Lanny will make sure of that after I'm gone.*

The fallen crystal emitted colors left and right, a kaleidoscope of nameless hues. Danny's legs were moving, taking him away, and he had no control over them. *I gotta go help Randy. Why am I getting further from him—*

Danny was running, running away, looking over his shoulder during his retreat. Lanny still hadn't managed to get up, and Danny could still hear the stomach-twisting *pow-crack* sound of his buddy's skull making contact with brick. *No one could survive that hard of a hit.*

Danny covered distance quickly without slipping, his vision blurred by tears, running faster than he'd ever run in his life.

Chapter Fourteen

The race home seemed to take just minutes. Danny stuck to the road for part of the way, but shortcut through an open field when the first engine came into earshot. It made Danny think about all the missing children he'd seen on the news. Was Lanny behind that? And if he was, why? What would possess him to do such a horrendous thing? If he had kidnapped them, were they still alive, perhaps locked in that lair from the pictures, starved, tired and waiting for the black goat of a thousand young to come eat them? Danny didn't know. He needed to dig deeper still. He wanted to know how old his grandma had been at the time of her death. He needed to know more about Lanny and the missing children, about the crystal and the monster from the photograph—a two-dimensional image that had succeeded in erasing any last trace of innocence in him. That's what Ethel's second purpose was, wasn't it? To take his innocence and life-force away by varying degrees? Even if there was a minor flaw in the answer, it felt right, and if something felt right, it had to be the truth. Because your heart never lied to you when your life was on the line. Never.

Danny jogged across fields, climbed over fences, received indifferent looks from cows. The sky darkened. The snow never stopped falling, and Danny never stopped moving.

He made it home in record time, disappointed to find the place empty. His mom's SUV was not in the driveway when he jogged up to the door, and it was not parked in the garage when he threw the door open. The inside felt warm and cozy; he could feel his capillaries burning under his skin.

"Mom? Dad?" he called out. No answer. The house felt empty, too.

He knew he needed to get in touch with his parents before Lanny did, because Lanny could resort to desperation.... if he hadn't already.

Danny then asked himself a question that made the house feel much colder and far emptier:

What if he does something to one of them?

They'd never know until it's too late.

***

Amy searched Ducougery several times over in search for her son. The steady snowfall had transitioned to a light blizzard and the air felt as cold as a meat locker. She switched the heater on full-blast as she turned the corner of Harbor Avenue the fourth... fifth... sixth... time?

Everybody in the neighborhood seemed to have retired to their homes to escape this hard winter in mid-fall. A lot of leaves clung steadfast to a lot of trees. Daylight savings wasn't for another week. *Eerie.*

She wiped at tears, sometimes smacking them angrily away, and tried unsuccessfully to stop her hands from shaking on the steering wheel. Hot air dried her eyes, making only more tears form.

At the bottom of Banter's Ridge, Amy sat staring up at a traffic light. In the gloom, it looked very bright, ruby red. Snow fell on every hanging wire, and wind blew them, blew everything, with unfeigned hostility.

Vehicles trundled through the intersection. Some went straight. Others turned left. Then, when her light turned green, she released her foot off the gas. The SUV trundled forward. Her hands spun the wheel, the tires turned, and her heart leaped into her throat when the scream of sirens filled her ears. An ambulance flew by, barreling up Banter's Ridge in a white blur. *Another inch over,* she thought, *and it would've scraped paint off my vehicle.*

Her foot lingered over the brakes, and her mind, a Swiss-cheese blob, slowly put two and two together. *My son. I can't find him, I called everybody, I looked everywhere, save Lanny's, and that's where this ambulance is heading.*

She didn't watch the traffic light change back to red; she floored the accelerator when a bright blue Mazda pulled out in front of her. The driver pushed on his horn, deafening the intersection with a blaring *huuuuuu!* Sweat popping from her pores, nerves jingling, she soared up Banter's Ridge, mentally linking the ambulance with her hurt or dying son. *Ambulances don't go that fast unless someone's in grave condition.*

She wasn't worried about losing control of her SUV on forming ice; wrecking was the least of her concerns. She simply needed to catch up to the ambulance and ride its tail until it reached its destination. That's what she did. Her speedometer reached 45 within seconds, then was up to 83 not much later. The vehicle slid once, maybe twice, but she never pumped the brakes. Her quivering foot hardly let off the gas at all.

Danny, please be well. I love you. I'm sorry I didn't believe you. I don't know what's going on, but that doesn't matter, all that matters is you're okay.

***

She followed, heart pounding, mind whirling, hoping earnestly that the ambulance went onward, past the mailbox labeled *Crowley*. It didn't. It turned where she dreaded it would, and her heart stopped beating altogether. Her lungs deflated. There were already two cop cars parked by the side of the house, lights flashing, four police men standing around, apparently waiting. Lanny was with them, running his hands through what little hair he had left on his head.

The ambulance came to a stop between the two police cruisers parked haphazardly in the driveway. Amy parked behind it. She got out of her SUV before they had time to open the back doors and pull out a stretcher.

"Where is he?" she belted out, ignoring the falling snow that

fell into her eyes as she charged forward. One cop, a real fatty, blocked her way, but she pushed past him, eyes burning, cold biting. "I wanna know where he is! What happened to my son? What did you do to him? Where is he?"

Her attention never veered from her brother. There was some blood smeared on his coat, his hands. He couldn't seem to look her in the eye.

"Where is Danny?" She was screaming.

Neighbors came outside to watch the drama unfold.

Officer Fatty grabbed her arm. "Look, Miss, you're gonna have to—"

She wrenched her arm out of his rough grip and struck Lanny's chest with her fist. "I want to know!"

"Miss!"

"No, Officer," Lanny said, "it's okay. She's my sister." Finally, he looked at her—but just barely and just temporarily.

She bit her tongue, shivering not just from cold but from nerves, too.

"It's okay, Amy. Danny's okay, I think."

"You think?" She struck him again, harder. He made no attempt at stopping her, just let her hit him over and over.

The paramedics rolled the stretcher down the hill, around to the back of the house. As she watched it go and waited for it to return with Danny's lifeless body on it, she found herself almost unable to stand. Danny was dead, he had to be, that's all there was to it, he was dead and gone, because why else would the authorities be out here the same day he went missing... after several days of odd, abnormal behavior?

"What did you do, Lanny? What did you and Ethel do!" she wailed.

"I didn't do anything. Calm down, Amy."

"You and her—my mother were behind this. Why is his—why do you have his blood all over you—"

"It's not... listen." He reached for her flailing hands. She pulled them away, struck again, and they played this little grab-and-slap game for awhile. The cop muttered something into his CB. The flashing strobe lights spun and spun, making the snow look translucent.

Amy eventually let Lanny take control of her hands, but when he tried to embrace her, she pushed him back and gave him a punch to the face. Officers subdued her. Officer Fatty wrapped her with a blanket. It felt warm; the monumental feeling of loss, however, felt exasperating.

See him. I have to see him one last time. See what this monster did to him.

"Was it your kid, Mam?" a cop asked. His glum tone made the knife in her chest twist. She threw the blanket to the ground, shoved Lanny with enough force to knock him down, and went running. *Danny!"*

"Wait, Miss!" The officer chased after her, but she outdistanced him. She passed by Lanny's Lincoln, rounded the corner of the house, and stopped when she saw the paramedics hoist the body up onto the stretcher. So much blood. An excessive amount of blood stained the snow red and blotched the base of the well out back.

My Danny...

The paramedics wheeled the body up the slope, toward her. The cop, meanwhile, grabbed her by the shoulder and pulled her out of the way.

"Danny!"

When the first EMT was out of the way, Amy looked down at the bloody, lifeless body on the stretcher. All the despair and anguish turned to instant relief, a pleasant wave of pure white elation that was stronger than any opiate. Danny wasn't laying there after all. It was his friend Randy, rendered incapacitated by a gruesome head injury. Part of his skull was missing. Part of his brain was poking out of the wound. Shocking, but not unendurable, because it wasn't *her* child.

"I tried telling you it wasn't him," Lanny said, wrapping the blanket around her again.

She turned and smacked him across the cheek. "You filthy... what did you do? Where is he?"

Four red lines slowly mantled Lanny's cheek. He didn't fluster. "He and his friend broke in. When I calmly tried to confront them, they reacted strangely, violently, even. They tried to climb onto the roof to get away. Randy fell, bumped his head, and Danny just ran away."

"Broke in? That's the biggest load of—"

"It's true, Miss." The officer was standing nearby, taking pictures of the scene. "We checked, and the lock was tampered with. The upstairs room was in shambles. Those boys were trying to rob the place."

She didn't believe a word of it. "No, he's lying." She pointed to Lanny.

"No, he's not, Miss," the officer shot back. "Got eyewitnesses from the neighbor. He wasn't here the whole time, but he saw the tail end of it."

"No. No!"

"Yes," Lanny said coldly. "I don't know what they were doing here, Amy, I honestly don't. That Randy kid was trouble. You know that. I think he coaxed Dan here for some reason."

"Randy's troubled, not trouble. And Danny hasn't done a bad thing in his life."

"Come on inside, I'll get you a cup of coffee. It's cold out here."

"No. What *were* they doing here? Tell me that."

"Like I said, I don't know. I opened Ethel's old room and they climbed out the window. I tried grabbing them so they wouldn't hurt themselves, fall off the roof or anything, and that's unfortunately what happened."

Amy took a step away from him. "I don't believe you."

Lanny stared at her. "What's the matter? Why are you looking at me like that? You're looking at me like I had something to do with all this."

"You don't know what Danny's been going through the last few days."

Lanny's stare grew duller, colder. "The only thing that's wrong is who he's hanging out with."

"I can tell you, Mam," the officer said, "that I've seen that boy quite a few times being where he's not supposed to, doing things he's not supposed to, and, if he survives, he's probably going to end up in jail for a long stint."

"Survives? He's not..." Amy looked at Lanny. His mouth had condensed into a fine line.

"Coma. He's in bad shape—"

"Very bad," the officer corrected.

"But he could pull through. Hit his head on the well when he jumped off. Then Danny darted away."

"It's a hundred percent true, Miss. Neighbors can vouch for everything he said."

Neighbors. I need to get more out of them. But not now, not with Lanny here, not with the police and paramedics here, but very soon. The sooner the better without being this minute.

In a couple, few hours, just to give this scene time to settle down a little.

"You haven't heard from Danny?" Lanny asked her. "What's been going on with him lately? You said—"

"It's not your concern. Ethel's death has taken a toll on him."

Lanny nodded slightly. "I bet it has."

"What does that mean?" Her voice was dry and dull.

He shrugged his shoulders. "I didn't mean anything by it. Nothing, okay? I love him too, he's my nephew."

"He's *my* son," she shot back.

"You two sound like a married couple," the cop joked, but neither Amy nor Lanny cracked a smile. "Mr. Crowley, is it okay if I ask you a couple more questions before I leave?"

"Sure." He looked down at the well. "I'm sorry for all this. When you see Dan, let me know he's okay, all right?"

"His name's *Danny*."

Lanny went to place a hand on her shoulder. As soon as his skin made contact with the fabric of her coat, she nudged it away. Then she stormed past him, back to her vehicle. One of the cop cars was gone, and the ambulance was screaming back down the long driveway. Amy got in her SUV. Suddenly, it all caught up to her. Her body shook—convulsed, actually—and the crying turned to an outright bawl. She didn't know where Danny was; he could still be hurt, in danger. And she knew, she knew without a shadow of a doubt that Lanny wasn't telling her or the cops the whole story—only the neighbors would do that.

Until then, she'd go home, see if Danny turned up, pray, hope for the best, and wait...

Wait until evening and come back.

Chapter Fifteen

He was home when she got there. She'd come into town nervous and high on adrenaline, worried there'd be an ambulance and some patrol cars parked in her driveway, too. She knew he was there before she walked in, for the lights in his bedroom were on. She didn't bother to open the garage door, either. She pulled up to the front door, driving over her lawn, unconcerned with leaving tire tracks behind.

"Danny!" she cried, getting out and shutting the door. She ran inside, leaving the front door open. Danny was standing at the other end of the hallway, head lowered, shoulders slumped, posture meek and timid.

"I thought I'd never see you again," she sobbed.

They ran for each other. As they did, her feet seemed to glide over the hallway carpet. When they embraced, her heart exploded, and memories of him passed through her like a celestial wind. Holding him was magical. It felt as if she'd birthed him again, and was seeing him for the first time, except now she knew everything she hadn't known, all those wonderful memories, those amazing experiences, from teething to potty training. She loved him more than anything. This time, she wasn't letting go, not for anything.

"Oh, Mom, I'm so sorry." He was crying with her.

"Don't be sorry, baby, I'm just glad you're okay."

"How did you know?"

"I saw the ambulance going up Banter's Ridge. I'd looked all around town and couldn't find you. I went to my brother's and I thought it was you they were going after."

"I am so sorry, Mom. So you know about Randy?"

She nodded. Tears blinded her. "Yeah, sweetie, he hurt himself really bad. The paramedic said he didn't know if he'd survive. He's in a coma now."

Danny withdrew from her, but she held on tight. "What?" he

said. "He's not dead? He hit his head so hard."

Attempting a try a levity: "Well, you know how your friend is, Danny. He's hard headed."

They laughed. They laughed and they cried. Danny resumed the hug.

***

"Does dad know?" Danny asked. They were sitting on the couch in the living room now. All remaining daylight was fading fast.

She nodded. "Yeah, I phoned him with my new cell on my way here. He should've been home by now." She reached over and turned on a lamp.

"You don't think something happened to him, do you?"

She offered a smile. "Your dad can take care of himself, I think. Honey, I'm so sorry I didn't believe you."

"You do now?"

"Sometimes you have to believe before you can see."

He nodded. His eyes grew wide with acknowledgment. "Exactly! That's what Randy said, too. He didn't notice her until I told him the whole story. He had to believe before he could see her. Believe in my story, I mean."

"I will say this. I don't have any idea what's going on here, I really don't, but we'll get to the bottom of it. I want you to tell me what you went to my brother's house for. And why. Did you two break in?"

"We didn't *break* in; Randy picked the lock. We were looking for clues, trying to find out who or what Grandma Crowley was."

"Did Randy put you up to this?"

Danny shook his head. "No. I went there myself, without him. I was going to smash a window or something, and he showed up without me knowing."

"Did you find anything?"

"Grandma was some kind of witch, Mom."

"Witch?" A sardonic smile stretched across her face, but she quickly recanted it.

"I got some proof." Danny took three photographs out of his pants pocket and handed them over.

She looked at them with inquiring eyes. The first showed Ethel spewing ectoplasm. The second showed the demon—which froze her for a moment. When she came out of a little spell, she looked at the one of Ethel holding a baby.

"That's me," she said. "That's definitely me she's holding."

"I know, but look at her. She's so old in that photo. Are you sure, dead-sure she was 103 when she died?"

"Her birth certificate might be in among her things that I have."

"Mom, if she's really older than 103, I seriously doubt the one you have is real."

"Why does it matter? Does it? That should be the least of our worries, don't you think?"

Danny looked quizzically at her. "I guess you're right. You are. But it's another piece of the puzzle, you know? Can't put everything together until you have all the pieces, right?"

She smiled and nudged him playfully with her shoulder. "That's my boy, so smart. You take after me, not dad."

He laughed. "Do you know how we can find out her age?"

"There's someone who I work with. Name's Shawna. A computer whiz. She'd know."

"What's Ethel's maiden name?"

"Crowley. She dropped grandpap's name after he died. Don't know why, though. Come to think of it, she didn't talk much about him after that, either. When he was gone, she just went on with her life like nothing happened."

"Is there a reason why the front door is hanging wide open?" David shouted from the hall. Amy and Danny craned their heads. The front door shut with a bang. Footsteps approached, getting

louder, closer.

Amy got up and wrapped her arms around him. Even he looked like a stranger in her eyes.

"Everything okay?" he wondered.

She nodded and kissed him on the cheek. "Now, yes."

He moved her out of the way. "Danny, what do you think you're doing leaving school, roaming around, doing god knows what with god knows who?"

"David," Mom said, "don't."

"Don't? He worried me sick. Worried you sick. Don't you think—"

"No," she interrupted, "I don't think. And neither should you."

"What? What are you talking about, Amy?"

She narrowed her eyes. "It's real."

"What's real?" he shot back.

"What Danny said happened. About the hallucinations, about Ethel."

He snickered and sighed and shook his head. Amy gazed at him.

"I'd expect it from him." David pointed to Danny. "He's a kid. But you?"

"Me, what? What, David? Tell me. I'm an *adult?* You know, you're in church with me once in a while. You believe in God. You believe in the bible, don't you?"

He sighed and shook his head. "That's different. It has nothing to do with what he thinks he's seen." He pointed to Danny again as if he were a misbehaving dog.

She felt her face warm, her anger rise. "Look, lay off him or get out. He doesn't need this."

"I strongly disagree. He does need this. Ever since he started hanging out with that kid, Randy Wayde..."

She raised her voice this time. "Randy, yes, the boy who might die."

He tilted his head back and laughed. "Oh my goodness, what

are you talking about?"

"He's in a coma, David! That's all you need to know."

"Why? Why is that all I need to know? How about our kid needing to be in school and not ditch with some delinquent?"

She let go. *"Because he and Danny went to my mother's house. Randy hurt himself, busted his head open, understand? The paramedics wheeled him by me on a stretcher, okay? I could see his brains. His blood was everywhere in the snow. Following me?"*

Jeering confusion permeated David's face, making him look both dumb and callous. "Why? What were they doing there? What happened?"

"He fell off the roof, Dad," Danny said, his voice shaky and high.

"That's right. Our son watched his friend almost die, and you're acting like this."

"Acting like what? I'm sorry about your friend, Danny, I am, but why were you there? What were you two doing there? Why did you leave school and mouth off to the principal?" His voice was rising.

Amy took Danny by the wrist and pulled him to his feet. "Come on, let's go." She pulled him out of the room and led him down the hallway.

"Wait!" David bellowed. "Where are you going? Come back here!"

"We'll come back," she said, "when you get your head on straight."

"My head is on straight!"

She ushered Danny into the loft below. "Mom, you're hurting me."

She relaxed her grip. "Sorry, but you're not getting out of my sight, honey. Not after all that." Her voice was almost cracking. "Sit down. I'm gonna call Shawna, and together we're gonna find out when my mother was born, okay?"

He sat. He nodded. He turned the TV on. It was kind of loud, so he turned it down.

Amy pulled a new cell phone out of her pocket. Her shaking fingers dialed, and Danny sat there, watching her more than the TV. *He must think I'm having a nervous breakdown...*

And I just might be...

"Hello?" Shawna's voice came through, sounding cheery.

"Shawna," Amy said, sounding desperate.

"Amy, is everything okay?"

Okay? I might never be okay again after today. I'm sure Danny feels the same. He looks like something the cat dragged in. Me too, if I ever look in a mirror.

"I need you to do me and my son a *huge* favor. Tonight, now, if you can. It's a matter of life and death. I wish I could explain it to you, but there's too little time. Too much has happened. Please, Shawna."

Shawna's voice went from sunny to grim really quick. "Anything. I'll need to know what it is or what it involves, at least."

"Those computer programs you have at work."

"Home, too. Do you need information on somebody? Can't you give me some more?"

"Yes, I need to know something. It's regarding my late mother. That's all I can tell you for now until we get the knowledge my son and I need."

There was a pause. Danny focused his attention on the TV, and Amy took notice. A haggard-faced witch with a big, hooked nose filled the screen. She told a distraught man to dig up something in a pumpkin patch. Obviously seeing enough, Danny turned off the TV.

"Okay, I'll boot up my computer. You come on over."

"My son's coming too, is that okay?"

"That's fine. See you soon."

Amy hung up the phone and smiled at her boy. "Get your coat.

I'll grab the keys. We're gonna get this figured out once and for all."

Chapter Sixteen

The blizzard continued as night fell over town. Streetlamps bathed the snow-covered ground with an ugly yellow-gray luminescence. Falling white flakes glistened everywhere. Wind howled steadily, like a disembodied coyote.

The drive to Shawna's took fifteen minutes, and during that time, Amy half-expected something bad to happen: a blown tire, a wreck, a stalling engine, what have you. To her surprise, nothing happened. They even got there without running into any traffic.

Shawna's house, a small, quaint condominium, stood at the beginning of Acre's Lane, preceding a long line of dapper homes. The yards were pathetically small and well-lit by arc-sodium lights. It was quiet here tonight; the only movement consisted of drifting snow and shadows passing from one side of a lit window to the other.

Shawna answered on the first knock. She was a short, petite woman who wore clothes that looked three sizes too big for her. Her eyes were blue, the color of sapphire.

"Hey, Amy, come in. This your son?"

They entered. Amy said, "Yeah, this is Danny, Danny, Shawna."

They shook hands. She offered him a hospitable smile. "Hello, Danny." Her teeth looked bleached and perfectly straight.

"Hi," he said shyly.

"Let me take your coats."

"No," Amy said, "we can't stay long. Hectic, Shawna."

Shawna frowned. "Come on down this way."

She led the way, and they followed. Amy had never been here before. There were pictures of Shawna and her family on both walls, and judging by the number of them, she either had a lot of relatives or knew somebody who loved photography. Each one was razor-straight and perfectly placed, but they were hard to see in the hall's gloom. Shawna entered a room at the end on the right. She flicked a switch, and bright light vanquished the darkness. The computer desk was positioned by the only window, along with a treadmill nearby, and a closet. The carpeted floor had zero signs of wear. The window overlooked a vacant alleyway covered with tire tracks.

Shawna pulled two folding chairs out of the closet, opened them, and placed them on opposite sides of the computer chair. They all took a seat. Then Shawna looked at Amy and said, "Is everything okay? You had—*have* me worried."

"I can't tell you yet, but I will when we get this straightened out. Okay?"

Shawna turned back to her computer and grabbed the mouse. She clicked it, and the screen added additional light to their faces. "What are you interested in me looking up? You said it had to do with your mother Ethel?"

"Yeah. I need you to find out when, precisely, she was born. Her birth records, her lineage, all that stuff."

Shawna looked inquisitively at them. Amy had never seen such deeply-creased brows on someone so young, and Shawna was only thirty-four. "What? Why would—"

Amy interrupted, "Please, I'll tell you the why after we find out the when." She was stern.

Without saying another word, Shawna turned back to her computer. It was an Apple that looked like it'd come from the year 2110. Hardly made a sound. And it responded quickly when she typed and clicked the mouse.

"Ethel Roselyn Crowley was her name," Amy informed. "She died suddenly at the age of 103, so I'd thought, but she may be older."

Shawna's fingers moved lightning fast, with cat-like precision. "Anita Carolyn Pellingser was her mother, and Fredrick Crowley was her father?"

"Yes. That's right." Amy sighed. "She was born in Rochester,

Rhode Island, so I've been told."

Shawna did some digging and brought up some records. A mountain of text filled the large flat-screen monitor. "Okay, yes, she was born in Rochester, Rhode Island in 1916 at Kerrington Hospital—"

Amy stopped her. "I know this. I think these are false records, though."

Shawna looked back at her and smiled. "Okay, okay, no worries. It could very well be fraudulent information tossed in to occupy the public records... but let's see what we can find when we use my program and filter the results. You know, a lot of people think that just because they get information online, it's true, but that's never been close to accurate. Everybody lies. The news lies. Politicians lie. Actors lie... but *they* do it for theatrics, entertainment."

"How does this thing work?" Danny asked.

"This H-7 program? Well, with it, I can access the deep web, go beyond what most people can. For instance, the internet is like the surface of the ocean; the deep web is under the water, so to speak."

Shawna typed in: hidden records of Ethel Roselyn Crowley. Then she clicked on a tab and narrowed the results. "Did Ethel or her parents have any nicknames?"

"Yes, Ethel's was Anuaka."

"Hmm." Shawna moved the mouse. "That's a gypsy word, I believe."

"Gypsy?" Danny asked.

"Yeah, it's—wait, hold on, I'm in the Classified Records site now. While what I'm doing is not completely legal, I told you I'd do this. Anything for a friend."

"That's not bad," Danny said. "I know kids at school who'd kill for this software."

Shawna smiled. "Shh. Between just the three of us.

The computer speakers belted out a loud *ding,* and a loading bar shot onto the screen. When it was finished loading—just seconds—a series of old pictures and text appeared.

They leaned in toward the computer monitor at the same time, like one combined being. Shawna read. Shawna read aloud and Amy couldn't believe what flowed into her ears.

"The Crowley family, the first great gypsy order in Romania, comes from a long linage of fortune tellers and mystics who many believed were simply con-artists and frauds looking to profit from the bereaved. But there are some very reputable people who've claimed to have experienced genuine phenomena performed by Fredrick Crowley. The most famous name on this list is Harry Houdini, who's reputed to have debunked several dozen psychic frauds during his lifetime.

"On the night of October 31, 1842, when Anita Pellingser gave birth to daughter Ethel Roselyn Crowley... wait a minute."

"1842?" Danny muttered.

"This definitely can't be right," Shawna said. "It's gotta be somebody else."

"No." Amy almost couldn't breathe. "Scroll down."

Shawna did. Under some more text, there was an old, worn photo of a couple holding a baby. "Oh, my god," Amy cried. "That's her. That's my mother."

Shawna narrowed her eyes as she looked at the screen. "That was taken in 1872, Amy. Couldn't be your mother."

Amy said, "Not unless she died... at the age of 146!"

Shawna looked at Danny, then at Amy, smiling sardonically. "What are you saying?"

"That's my mother! She was born in 1872. I believe she just won the Guinness Book of World Records for the longest-living person."

Shawna sounded doubtful: "How is that possible?"

Amy pointed to the screen. "I'm guessing that, if what this says is true, about gypsies and witchery, then maybe she found a way to sustain her life for quite some time."

Shawna looked at Danny and then back at Amy, confused and suspicious. "What?"

"You wanted to know why I needed your help on this, and this is it." Amy recounted the whole story from beginning to end, taking very few pauses in between, and looking to Danny whenever she came to parts she wasn't sure about. Shawna's expression changed several times during the telling of this tall tale, but even so, at the end, she never disputed anything Amy said.

After everything was on the table, Shawna said, "What are you going to do if all this is true?"

"I have no clue." Amy looked affectionately at her son. He was staring dumbly at the computer screen, so Amy turned to Shawna and said, "How much more is there? Can you print all this out? I'll pay you for ink and paper."

"Oh, yeah, don't worry about it. I'll print it out now."

She moved the mouse, clicked it a few times, and soon, the printer started its mechanical phase of making *clunking* noises and spitting out worded pages. As it did, Amy asked Shawna, "You probably think we're a couple of nutcases with this story, don't you?"

Shawna shook her head but didn't say a word. She kept her eyes on the printer, and that said enough.

When the printer stopped making its racket and puking out paper, Shawna handed Amy a thin sheaf that added up to five pages of priceless information. "We better get going; I don't wanna keep you, and I need to read this."

"I hope you and Danny'll be okay. Look, while I don't know if I believe this—I don't really know what I believe or don't believe—I know there's something else beyond this life. It's too mundane for this to be it. I don't pray, never have, but I'll try sending positive vibes your way."

"Thanks, Shawna," Amy said, giving her a little hug. After that, they left.

Amy was determined to finish where Danny had started by

going to Lanny Crowley's house and finding what he hadn't had time to. Whether Lanny was there or not wasn't a real concern to her; she had to do this for her son, and no brother of hers was going to stop her.

Nor the denizens of hell.

Or Ethel, her own mother.

Because a mother's love trumped them all.

Chapter Seventeen

While they headed home, Danny used the SUV's overhead light to read through some of the pages.

"It's believed by many, including the Society of Paranormal Research, that Harry Houdini has debunked in upwards of thirty-three mediums as actual frauds. But some doubters believe otherwise, speculating that the Crowleys were indeed the real deal.

It is known by many illusionists that, during many séances back at the turn of the twentieth century, mediums used false magic to shock and fool their customers. These ranged from simple parlor tricks to complicated contraptions. At one séance, Houdini, along with three other observers, watched in fascination as Fredrick Crowley levitated four inches off the solid ground simply by holding a crystal in his right hand. Claims state that this crystal, supposedly a relic from the Dark Ages, somehow gave him the power to defy gravity. One eyewitness reported that it glowed an *abnormal color* when he squeezed it. Another reported smelling a horribly foul odor, while yet another reported that the air suddenly felt *heavy*.

During this spectacle, Fredrick Crowley recited a strange language as if under spell, and bore his eyes on a specific spot in space. Houdini himself claimed that his eyes changed color briefly, to hues he could not describe and that made him cold. Several people were frightened by this entire display; one woman fled the room.

This presentation, it should be noted, was done in a locked room with sophisticated equipment and under close observation. Reporters who interviewed Harry Houdini in the days ahead said that he'd found no evidence of fraud, and yet couldn't explain how Crowley managed to float off the ground at all. Some believed he changed his story later on because of fear or ridicule, but others think he was threatened by the very powers Crowley seemed to possess.

Whether what happened in that room was true magic or just fraud, nobody really knows, but there have been wild claims regarding the Crowley family. Some mediums have said that they are descendants of demons or demigods or dark deities, just as the fabled Merlin was. A few religious zealots have claimed that they are simply a family of alchemists who'd found the elixir of life. Some skeptics still think this was no more than a parlor trick made to look authentic, and that Harry Houdini had never been there to begin with. The truth may never be known, and the mysteries of the Crowleys may never be revealed.

It's been said that there are forces constantly at work around us, that the skies are filled with things we cannot see or tap into without the right conduits, and that space and time are merely illusions. These eternal forces never die; they can only change form and will forever impact life on earth. The Crowleys, like the Egyptians and their pyramids, the Druids and their Stonehenge, may have discovered the proper tools for harnessing the energy from these queer dimensions and unknown universes. And he who holds that key may be the most powerful being in all of creation."

It was a lot to take in. Too much, in fact. As soon as Danny stopped reading, silence became so prevailing, it was almost deafening. Amy didn't know what to say, and Danny didn't seem to, either. They both watched the road, watched the snow come down, watched the wipers swing from side to side, watched the headlights wash out the white road ahead. They finished going home in eerie, monotonous silence.

When they went in, nothing was said. Dad gave Amy a few inquisitive looks but kept his mouth shut, as Amy hoped he would. Danny went right to bed, or at least to his room, and shut the door behind him. Amy got a drink of orange juice from the fridge. Dad lingered in the hallway, staring at her—she could *feel* him leering—eager to engage in an argument she knew he couldn't win. When it came to maternal matters, she was always right, because a mother's love had no boundaries, no conditions, no end. There was a reason she'd carried him for nine months and David hadn't. Amy had seen how bad Danny had become lately. Now, David was the third wheel, the outsider who knew nothing and likely wouldn't until he chose to open his eyes and pay attention.

He stood there, watching. Amy thought she saw him open his mouth to say something before he simply threw up an arm and walked away. He spoke four words as he receded, grumbling them: "I'm goin' to bed."

The bedroom door shut pretty forcefully, and Amy now stood alone. Alone with too much arcane knowledge of stuff she couldn't begin to comprehend. Just who really were her ancestors? Why were they doing this to Danny, their own flesh and blood? What were the extraordinary things she'd seen in those old photographs? She couldn't wrap her head around it. She tried, but it came loose every time, unhinged by years and years of reality and normalcy. Maybe all ghost stories were based on fact from unknown times, strange people doing stranger things.

She sat on the couch in the living room, drinking her orange juice and waiting for the time to be right. Waiting for Danny and David to go to sleep. What she was going to do was probably dangerous, too, but she had a son to protect and a curiosity to fill.

She left the room dark, the TV off. Dim light from the kitchen cast distorted banister railing shadows against the wall she was facing. When vehicles drove past, their headlights blazed through the only window, brightening the room brilliantly before passing by. She was hardly aware of drinking the juice, much less holding the cup in her hands. At times she'd glance at her watch; at other times she'd check it religiously. The wonder was insatiable; she couldn't help herself. This was high-level voodoo stuff she was about to jump head-first into, and who better to learn from than the other last living descendant of Ethel—Lanny?

And what better place was there to jump into the Lion's den than ground zero: the house where she'd grown up?

She left at two in the morning. Neither Danny nor David left their rooms during that time, and she made sure to leave as quietly as possible so as not to wake them.

The snow was still falling in blizzard fashion. The streets and houses were bathed in yellow light and glistening. It would have been a lot more beautiful had it not been for all this paranormal bunk. But Amy figured the opposite was true, as well—*where there's happy hearts and ugly weather, there is beauty. True warmth and peace come from within every time.*

She backed out of the driveway. The vehicle slid a little, but she righted, shifted into drive, and coasted down Tinney Lane. At the first stop sign, she looked back at her house in the rear-view mirror. No one had come out and no lights had come on. The area looked dead.

She drove to her brother's on autopilot. The only thoughts she had while getting there, were as follows: *even if he catches me breaking in, he'll scold me but he won't hurt me. Lanny, of all the people on God's green earth, wouldn't harm or kill someone, much less his own sister.* Amy truly believed this. Never did she find this distinct thought foolish or misleading. She couldn't see him doing any more than smiling sarcastically.

She pictured the photo Danny had shown her of the demon standing in what looked like a makeshift dungeon. One wall in that cellar had had a cheap wooden panel attached to it—one she'd seen plenty of times in her life: Ethel's bedroom closet. It was exactly the same. She'd gone in there a hundred times while playing hide and seek as a kid. That meant only one thing: that apparent dungeon was located somewhere inside the house. And she was determined to find it.

She didn't know what she'd do when she found it, but finding it was another piece of the puzzle, as Danny would have said. Additionally, her curiosity was about to burst out of her like stars from an aerial fireworks shell. This had become an obsession, an addiction to uncover hidden truths about the world nobody knew.

She couldn't stop.

The lights were out in every window when she got there. Good. The house was engulfed in darkness. Good. She knew that Lanny had no video monitor equipment surveying the house—or at least that's how it had been for umpteen years. Her brother was probably asleep in bed. That was good, too. *That means the window in his room views the woods, not the front yard or the road.*

Amy coasted up the driveway, turning off the headlights seconds before they would cut through the front windows of the house. The TV in the living room wasn't on, as the flickering light, which she'd seen plenty of times before after coming home late, was quite noticeable at night. She made sure not to accclerate too much, either. The hum of her engine could awakened him, which was why she let the SUV creep its way toward the dark, cryptic house. It eventually stopped by the walkway that led up to the front door.

Amy examined the place, her childhood home, with timid eyes. It had lost every bit of sentimentality it once had. This house held dark secrets that involved the degradation of her own son. The thought of seeing it burn to the ground was satisfying.

Just what is she after Danny for?

A witch... my mother was a witch, and she's not even dead, after 147 years and being six feet underground.

She almost chuckled at the ridiculousness of the idea, but covered her mouth and discarded the thought.

Amy opened her door gently and quietly. Slowly, she stepped out into the strong, biting wind. The ground beneath her shoes was slick, and she slid a spell before clutching onto the door to regain her footing. When she did, she proceeded.

Amy left her door open as she walked toward the house she used to regard as a castle. She had good, warm memories of this place, which had soured greatly over just the past few days. This house stared back down at her tonight, a virtual demon she wanted to understand but had to dread. There was a room somewhere in there she'd never known about until tonight, always there, locked away, hidden, and she'd passed it by thousands of times without knowing it was there. How could her mother have buried it for so long? How could she have done that?

Amy tried the knob, and got what she expected: a locked front door. That was okay, though, because she knew where Lanny hid the spare key: in a fake rock underneath the window. Then it occurred to her that he could have hidden it somewhere else after Danny and Randy had broken in.

Bad idea. I shouldn't have come here at all. This was a mistake.

But it's too late to turn back now.

The fake rock was still there, halfway submerged in the snow. Amy leaned down and picked it up. It was so light, she wondered how tonight's wind hadn't carried it away into the woods or somebody else's yard.

She closed her eyes. Squinted them shut. With a shivering hand, she turned it over. Though it was dark, there was enough light to reveal what she'd feared: no key. No way inside. Botched try, she told herself, tossing the rock back onto the ground. She glanced at the rock as it sat in the snow, turned away, and then turned back. A glint of dirty yellow had winked back at her. So when she knelt down to get a better look, she realized there was something brass jutting up through a layer of snow. Amy reached down. Her fingertips brushed against cold, hard metal. The key. It had fallen out of its hiding place, was all. *See? Stressed for nothing.*

She picked it up. It slid into the locking mechanism with ease. It turned the tumbler with a *clanking* sound that felt good in her hand. She tossed the key aside and grabbed the knob. Holding her breath, she turned it as slowly as she felt was necessary, and felt it give. Like that, she was inside.

Darkness greeted her. Tonight seemed especially dark, though, the air hard and heavy and disquieting. If not for the light from the cable box and a nightlight in the kitchen, it would've been pitch black.

She closed the door behind her, not completely, just enough to block out the cold and not be thrown open by a mean gust of wind.

The place would have sounded like a tomb had it not been for the grandfather clock ticking and the constant howl of wind outside. Together, they made a foreboding clamor.

Amy crept forward. She didn't really need a ton of light to see, anyway; she knew this room as well as she did the back of her hand. The clock stood a few feet to the right. A wall about a foot to the left. The bathroom was straight ahead, and the kitchen through the small hall around it. That was where she commanded her feet to take her, and that's where they did.

The blue light over the kitchen sink produced just enough luminosity to show you where everything was inside. The fridge stood beside the sink; the table stood beside a wall covered with tacky wallpaper she had never liked but her mother had always loved. The window, the only one in the room, presented a clear view of the well out back. Amy looked out this window. She cringed when she saw faint traces of Randy's blood in the snow; it was no longer liquid but had turned to twinkling red crystals over the past several hours. She asked herself if he'd survive before wondering how Danny felt about it. How would he cope without his best friend, his only friend, and the unseen evils that were after him?

Amy looked into the woods, at the well, into the black ring, wondering if it held any answers. She had grown calm over the last minute or so, not feeling any sense of danger, when her eyes refocused on something new in the reflection of the glass. At first she thought, a bug, one perhaps looking for shelter from the cold. She refocused her eyes, to the kitcheny world behind her. And there, standing behind her, was the black outline of a figure. Her heart went from a dull 10 MPH to a good 100 within the span of a second. Whoever or whatever was there wrapped a strong arm around her neck. She struggled, the surprise still registering. The assailant then shoved a rag drenched in strong-smelling stuff over her nose and mouth. Her mind began to reel, and her struggle swiftly died out. Before she lost consciousness, she heard a voice, one that sounded lucid, then faint. It said, calmly, sadistically, "Welcome home, Sis."

Chapter Eighteen

Danny hardly ever woke up in the middle of the night. He usually peed before bed and woke up the next morning without incident—save for his recent brushes with Crowley, that was. So, for him to open his eyes now, at 3:00 a.m., without a lingering evil presence in the room to disturb him, was quite abnormal.

And equally as disturbing, there wasn't a sleepy cell or muscle fiber in him.

Uh-oh.

He thought she had woken him—the woman with the power to summon the black goat of a thousand young.

His eyes flitted about the room. Nothing maniacal in sight, so that was good. Just the same ordinary things. The important thing was, *he* didn't feel like he was in danger. He didn't *feel* like a bad presence was near... but he did feel it elsewhere, as if some heart-string had been touched or stepped on or even trampled on. And the first thought he had was of his mother. The visualization of her in his mind provoked feelings of loss and sadness. He couldn't understand it, but he had to check on her, see if she was all right.

Danny got out of bed, fully awake, fully alert. His window cast a reflection on his door and part of the wall. Tiny dots—snow—could be seen descending diagonally. He rushed out of his room and down the hall to his parents'. The door was ajar, and he, before opening it to its fullest, knew he wouldn't find her in bed. And she wasn't. His mother was gone.

Don't panic. She's probably downstairs, getting a drink, or farther down the hall, in the bathroom.

These happy thoughts felt more like hopes rather than possibilities. His instinct told him, declared: *your mom isn't anywhere in this house. She's not here at all. Something's happened to her, and you're the only one who knows it.*

Danny checked the house anyway. He searched upstairs first.

The bathroom was empty, the lights out, the door wide open. Every other room revealed the same. When Danny went downstairs, he searched every room, turned on every light, looking, checking twice before finally going out to the garage. Her SUV was not there.

The last place he checked was outside. Her SUV was not in the driveway, yard, or parked by the curb.

Where did she go?

The better question might've been: *where has she been taken?*

This thought upset the happy ones, and inside, at the very core, it felt like the truth. His mother was in trouble or dead.

"Get a grip on yourself," he said, slinking back inside, locking the door, and sitting down on the living room couch. He sat timidly, head down, eyes lowered, shoulders slumped, hands together, feet askew. He sat in the darkness, thinking horrible things a kid wasn't supposed to think. His mother lying in a casket, all dolled up but dead. His dad sobbing uncontrollably. The pallbearers carrying her coffin to a hole in the ground. Them lowering her six feet under. The priest saying, "Ashes to ashes, dust to dust." Them bowing their heads to say a prayer. People crying. Relatives putting their hands on his shoulders and him too pained to deal with physical human contact and pushing them away. Everybody leaving the cemetery. Then, before the limo taking off down the road, him looking back through the rear windshield and seeing Grandma Crowley standing there, grimacing, pointing, laughing, the bugs pouring from her face. Her body hovering many feet above the solid ground. Looking at him with black, evil eyes.

It could happen, too, that was the crazy thing about it. What couldn't happen, after all he'd been through? What *bad* couldn't take place? You turned on the news, and what did you see? Killings, starvation, climate change, death, war, suffering. Danny had heard it somewhere—that if the devil was real, then it stood to reason that God was real, too. If so, where? Where was He? On vacation? Was it permanent? There seemed to be far too much pain and sorrow in the world for there to be any likelihood of miracles.

Was God dead?

Did He exist at all?

Were good souls, positive spirits, the reverse Ethel Crowley's—where were they hiding? Why weren't they helping him?

What could he do to stop her?

He knew he had only days remaining, and that his mother may have had none.

"Danny?"

He almost jumped out of his seat.

He whipped his head around, bracing for the worst.

But it was only his dad, not Ethel. "What are you doing down here this late? Why are you crying?"

He hadn't known he was. He wiped the tears away and said, "Mom's gone."

"Where? Where did she go? Tell me."

What do I tell him? I speak the truth and I'll get yelled at. Disbelieved.

"Well?" His dad sounded scared. Danny detected a fear in his tone that he'd never heard before. His eyes were wide, glistening.

"I... She's... I..."

"Tell me, Danny. Do you know where she is?"

Immediately, he shook his head.

"I'll go see if her car's in the gar—" He turned to walk away, but Danny stopped him.

"No, it's not there. I already checked."

David's voice cracked as he said, "Come on, I know you know something. I'm getting kind of worried. Tell me what's going on."

"I don't *know* where she is, honest."

And it was the honest answer. Better and more accurate, hopefully, than saying the black goat got her.

"Then why are you up at this time of night?" Dad said. "Crying? In the living room? With the lights out? And how did you know to check on her?" He sat beside him on the couch.

"We both found out what's going on," Danny told him. "About Ethel. About what I saw. The so-called nightmares."

Dad stared at him silently. "What did you find out?"

"She's a witch who was 147 years old when she died. She's—"

Dad ran a hand through his hair as if he were trying to take it all off in one slow, deliberate movement. "Danny, be serious now. Where is your mother?" The anger was evident, coming, building.

"Pictures," Danny said, remembering them. "I have pictures that'll convince you!"

Danny got up, but dad grabbed his arm before he could walk away. "No. Not pictures. The truth. I want to know what is going on, and I want to know this very—"

Danny wrenched his arm away with such force, he tripped, fell, and banged his head against the coffee table. When he looked back up, his dad spun in circles.

"Danny? Danny, are you okay?"

The anger in his voice had been replaced with pity.

Danny felt dizzy as he got up, but he refused to let his dad get near him again. The adult had to get it through his thick, cynical head that all this was real, no questions asked.

"Pictures—"

"Would you stop with the pictures? You're bleeding." His dad stepped closer. Danny took two steps away. "No! No! I'm not saying another word, because if I do, you're only going to get mad and tell me to stop telling lies, when it's the truth!"

"Danny, stop this!"

"No! You stop it, *David!*"

His dad stopped advancing and stumbled a little. In all his fourteen years, he'd never—not that he could recall without giving it some careful thought—mouthed off to his father like this. David was taken so aback, he retreated a few steps. Pain furnished his features. The anger had soured into something easier for Danny to deal with.

"I swear on my soul, to God, I don't know where mom is. But I do know she's in some sort of trouble."

David stood there, unblinking, not moving, seemingly not breathing. Danny gazed into his eyes, not turning away. He felt very hot, physically and emotionally. He was insistent that his father was not going to pass it off this time, no, not *this* time. If he didn't listen, didn't open his eyes, their whole family was in a world of trouble.

Dad knelt down. Danny steeled.

"Where do you think she is, Danny? Hmm?"

The *hmm* came out arrogantly. Danny didn't falter; he stood his ground and kept eye contact. "I. Don't. Know."

David struck the wall with his palm, hard enough to dent the drywall. There it was, Anger's return. But when Danny didn't flinch, didn't gasp, didn't even blink, David's reaction shifted to utter disbelief. The kind when you see a magic trick performed and can't figure it out.

"We gotta go find her, Dad. I know something's happened."

Dad touched the dented wall, ran his hand against it, and nodded. "If you're lying... go get the pictures you mentioned. I need you to tell me everything. Everything, okay? 'Cause I'm worried now. And hurry. It's three in the morning."

"Okay. I'll be right back."

***

The refrigerator hummed quietly in the background as they sat on the floor in the living room, going over it all. Danny showed him the pictures and told him everything he knew.

"So, you think Ethel's a witch who's come back from the dead to take you to hell?"

Danny stared him down. "Yes."

153

Dad laughed. "I always knew she was a witch, just not the kind who rid on brooms and stirred pots."

"She doesn't do that."

"But she can cast spells and give you nightmares, am I right?"

"You saw the... look at the picture!"

Dad refused to look at it again. He pushed it away whenever Danny presented it to him.

"You can manipulate a photo easily with Photoshop."

Danny threw the picture. It spun through the air before landing face-up on the carpet. "I didn't manipulate it! This is real!"

"If you had any idea—any—where do you think she could be? What do you think could've happened to her?"

Danny finally looked away, distraught. "I don't know. I wish I did, but I don't. My only guess is that Ethel took her away."

"To where?" Dad said doubtfully.

Something in Danny's head clicked, or shifted, as he added two memories together. He recalled Randy saying something about the *wooden panel* when they were going through Ethel's belongings. Yes, he'd seen that panel of wood before, too, in the photograph of the demon. That wooden panel had been part of the inside of Ethel's closet.

I'd do anything to protect you,

he also remembered his mom saying. So what if Ethel hadn't abducted her and taken her to some far-off wasteland? What if Mom had gone straight to the source to learn more, figure it all out, and perhaps put an end to it? There was only one place to go, wasn't there? Lanny's house. Ethel's previous home. The place where Randy had basically lost his life, if not at least, his brain?

"Lanny's..." he muttered.

"Uncle Lanny's?" his dad reiterated. "You think he took her?"

"No. I think she may have went there herself."

"Why?"

"For me."

David said he'd call, but Danny flat-out told him no, that it was too dangerous, that they had to drive out there themselves. When David insisted, Danny took the phone out of his hand and smashed it with his heel. At first he pleaded with his father, then raised his voice, until, eventually, he commenced to throw the worst temper tantrum of his life.

And Danny didn't stop until David complied.

***

During the drive, Danny felt like the parent, and dad seemed like the child. He'd made him do something he didn't want to do—force him into believing a child's horror story he did not want to take seriously.

It was so dark that night, and quiet, the wipers on full speed. Traffic was almost non-existent. Everyone was nestled in their warm homes, sleeping, having pleasant dreams, probably, while he was here trying to face his nightmarish reality.

Surprisingly, the car didn't slide much on the bad roads, and by the time they reached the end of Lanny's driveway, Danny told his dad to turn off the headlights, which he did.

They coasted slowly down a long, narrow pathway bordered by snow-covered shrubs.

The three front windows of the Crowley House were burning with light, so that meant somebody was up.

But it was something else that gave them a jolt.

Mom's car. It was parked in the driveway, unattended to.

"Well I'll be," dad groaned. "You were right."

"Just hurry up and park. We gotta find mom before it's too late."

"Danny, I'm sure she's fi—Danny!"

Danny was out of the car and gone before his father could stop or even pump the brakes. He left the door hanging open as he ran toward the house.

Careful, he thought. *Do this the way ninjas do it. Don't break the door down and make a ton of noise; sneak in and get Lanny by surprise.*

Danny forgot about his father; he put his sole focus on his mother and tried the windows instead of the front door. None of them opened. They were all locked, and after skirting the entire perimeter, Danny found that the place was sealed tight. There was no getting in without either using a key or making a lot of commotion.

"Danny!" his dad yelled.

Danny turned and shushed him. His father had parked and was just getting out of the car.

How do I get in? How do we get inside?

Snow blinded him, stinging his eyes, falling into his mouth, making him cold and wet. Trees swayed from side to side in the wind, snow drifting off their boughs in bountiful supply. There was light in every window of the Crowley house, no slinking shadows or anything, but bright tungsten light shining in every corner of the place. Danny knew he had the advantage in that department, because the darkness could conceal him. He'd be able to spot Lanny's shadow long before Lanny would spot his... even though that wasn't very reassuring anyway. Danny was just scared, both for himself and his mom, who could be dead by now. He had to find a way in, even if that mean breaking a window.

Danny picked up a rock. It was heavy and cold and slippery in his hand. Lurching forward, he went to throw it through the nearest window, but David grabbed the crook of his elbow seconds before the stone took flight. It slipped out of his hand and landed on the walkway.

"What do you think you're doing?" Dad sounded furious.

"She's in danger."

"How do you—"

"Would you stop asking questions? I just know, Dad. For once, *for once,* trust me on this. Please?"

Dad shook his head. He calmly but briskly walked over to the front door, where a key was sticking out of the lock.

"Wouldn't it be better if we just turned this instead?"

Danny hadn't seen the key there, and felt stupid for having missed it. But that didn't matter now. They had a way in, a means of skulking like ninjas, and so that's what they did.

Quietly, they crept into the house, Danny leading, dad falling behind. It felt like a sauna inside, as if Lanny had turned the thermostat up to 90 degrees. Did it have something to do with Ethel or her spirit or the black goat of a thousand young? Danny didn't know, but his cold skin began warming back up quickly.

Quiet, too. The grandfather clock ticked, ticked, ticked. Danny found no obvious sign of a struggle. Nothing had been knocked over; blood was not running down the walls, thank God. It actually felt deserted to Danny, as empty as a tomb.

He walked through the living room, peeked into Lanny's study, and then into the bathroom. Too much light, too much heat, and not enough noise or company.

Danny made his way into the kitchen. There, he found nothing out of sorts. When he turned back to his father, he noticed that he hadn't followed him inside. "Dad?" he whispered loudly.

He received no response, at least not in the vocal sense. He could, however, hear his dad walking up the stairs to Ethel's old bedroom. Those rackety steps moaned and grunted all through the house.

Oh boy. If Lanny and mom are in here, surely they're gonna hear it.

Danny looked out the back window. Randy's blood had frozen to the well and ground, a sickening, heartbreaking sight to him. He pictured old, moldy hands reaching up from the depths of that well, climbing their way to the surface. A moment later, he remembered the coppery stench that always wafted up from that bottomless black hole, and thought:

Blood smells like copper.

"Ayho!" his dad shouted from upstairs. His voice sounded

muffled and rattling, yet likely loud enough to wake neighbors in a more suburban setting. Danny cringed. He backpedaled, turned, and banged his knee against the table chair. Dull pain radiated up his leg. He rubbed it where it hurt and cursed his dad for being so loud.

They're somewhere here, mom and Lanny, I know it. I can almost smell his cologne. I can smell her shampoo.

"Ayho!" dad called again. Danny looked up at the ceiling and thought about yelling, telling him to shut up and help him find a hidden button that opened a secret door.

He also thought about the wooden panel from the picture. In Ethel's room. If indeed there was a secret room in this very house, perhaps concealed in these walls, then didn't it stand to reason that it existed either above or below ground?

Couldn't be any attics, he thought. *This house isn't that tall, even with the two-stories.*

But what about a basement?

There had to be one, didn't there?

Of course. Why not? Devils supposedly lived underground. They rose from the depths of the earth, didn't they? That's where dungeons—like the one in the photograph—were located, too.

Danny looked at the tiled floor with creased brows. He jumped up and down on it, using just the balls of his feet. It squeaked and creaked and bowed with every impact, old grumpy floorboards unequipped for such strenuous activity.

A moment later he got down on his knees and put his ear against the floor, listening. Silence. Even the steady tick of the clock seemed to have died out. He had no idea where his dad had gone, but he wasn't making any noise now, and Danny worried about him, too.

"Dad?" he said, looking back. "Mom?" he said, looking down.

What if Lanny's got em? Got em both? And I'm the last—

Cool air stopped his train of thought. It was coming from his left, underneath the kitchen table, a chill draft. Creasing his brows further, Danny crawled under the table, bumping his head against one of the legs en route to the draft of cold air. It was a little difficult to see with the table blocking the light source, but he thought he could see a gap in the woodwork between the floor and the wall.

He waved his hand over this crack. Definitely, there was a space spewing air. Couldn't be from outside, either, because this wall directly faced the living room. *Did I find it?*

Danny wedged his fingers underneath the panel and pulled. The cheap wood bent, bowed, and started to crack. His fingers started to ache. His heart burned with hope and his mind ignited with curiosity as the wood bowed some more before eventually snapping. The sudden report sounded like a gunshot. Splinters pricked his palm. He didn't flinch or anything. And, upon looking into the crevice, he found himself staring at the same type of wooden panel from Ethel's bedroom closet. It was hidden beneath the kitchen wall, dirty, scuffed, and covered with webbing. A chunk of the paneling was missing, leaving a softball-sized hole. And through that hole, light shined... light which illuminated an underground room.

There is a basement!

But it was quiet.

Dead quiet.

There was no movement, either.

"Danny, what did you do!"

The sudden voice startled him so badly, he got up and hit his head against the underside of the table.

"Why are you breaking things? You just—"

Danny backed out from underneath the table and looked up at his dad. "There's a basement. Down here."

"What? Nobody's here, Danny, and stop these charades. I'm—"

Danny didn't want to hear any more. He got up, moved the table out of the way, and booted the wall with the heel of his shoe.

His dad tried to stop him, halfheartedly, but when the second, more powerful kick broke the plaster, David finally shut his trap and took notice.

They gazed through a hole, one which revealed a staircase that led down to a basement below. The top of this staircase began where the nook which contained the fridge, ended. Danny felt the need to kick again, not only as a means of entry, but to release some pent-up aggression.

Dad stopped him. "No, look out."

Danny moved aside. David squared up with the fridge, which hummed cozily. Its sleek surface cast his reflection. He squatted, maybe three inches, and hugged it. Using all his strength, David attempted to pull it out from its place. Couldn't.

"Heavy?"

"It's a refrigerator. Weighs a ton."

"Maybe there's a lever, or a switch somewhere."

They both searched for one.

After coming up empty-handed, Danny said, "Why don't we keep kicking that place out—"

The fridge, or something behind it, spat out a strange and curious sound. It sounded mechanical, like a car window rolling up loudly. David jumped back. Danny slid out of the way as the Maytag came out of the recess of the wall like a robot fresh off the assembly line. Then it turned to the side. Behind it was not a wall but an open archway where a wall had been seconds ago. In this archway stood Lanny with a black revolver in his hand and blood on his apron.

"David," Lanny said. "No sudden movements. Both of you, come down here." The gun wasn't shaking; Lanny held it in calm, restrained hands. Danny saw no agitation in his uncle, who had obviously done this before on a number of occasions. This wasn't new to him at all.

"Look," David said, or began to say, when Lanny cocked the firearm and aimed it at Danny. The feeling of having that thing aimed in his direction disturbed every nerve and froze his beating heart. The fact that it could go off at any time, even accidentally, was a torturous concept. The antithesis of stark comfort.

"I'm not going to ask you again, David." Lanny steeled his voice. And maybe for the first time, in Danny's experience, Lanny didn't seem so awkward.

This is his normal, Danny thought.

David paused. Danny wasn't sure if he didn't know what to do or how to react, or if he was debating on lurching forward and attacking Lanny.

"Okay, we're going. Come on, Danny," David said in a quivering voice.

David went down first, Danny second, Lanny third. The rackety steps bowed under their feet, making their footfalls sound loud and snappy. At the bottom, Danny saw the makeshift dungeon he'd seen from the photos. Odd symbols written in rusted blood covered the dirty walls, and animal bones littered the floor. Against one wall stood a rack chocked full of whips, chains, blades and other sundry implements of torture. The ceiling teemed with beams, pipes, webbing, more speckles of dried blood. Six dim bulbs shed light from different directions. In the darkest corner stood the altar, to which mom was tied.

She was on her knees, hands clasped together, wrists bound in handcuffs, dirty, bruised and cut up. Seeing her this way sparked a fury inside him that made him want to rip Lanny's head off and spit down his neck. She looked petrified, shaking, sobbing, whimpering. Gashes covered her face. One eye had swollen shut. Her bottom lip was hanging.

"You..." David turned to Lanny, but Lanny quickly responded by sticking the barrel of the gun against his head.

"Don't try it. For your wife's sake. For your son's sake. You don't want to leave her a widow, do you? Or Dan an orphan?" Lanny wasn't playing, wasn't bluffing. Danny could almost sense that.

The room reeked of old copper.

"What are you going to do with us, Lanny?" Dad said condescendingly.

It took Lanny forever to reply to this. "I haven't decided. Obviously I can't let you go now. Either I'll have to keep you or kill you."

"Why?" Dad gulped. "Why are you doing this?"

"Hey, it's not what I want. I never wanted this. I'd do just about anything to have had another mother growing up, one who hadn't showed me things, done things, become things I never wanted to be."

"Doesn't God give free will?"

Lanny paused. "That's the problem, David. He gave my mother free will. And with that, she turned me into the monster I am."

"You don't have to do this."

"Please, let us go," mom pleaded. "Let Danny go. He's got nothing to do with this."

Lanny was taken aback. He smiled uncomfortably. "Nothing to do with this? Nothing to do with this? Danny has *everything* to do with this. Don't you think I thought our mother died a few days ago? I thought—I hoped that was the end of this waking nightmare, but it wasn't. It was just the beginning. All this time, and just the beginning. Can you believe it?" He laughed sardonically.

"The well..." Danny muttered. "The coppery smell out back in the well. Dead children. That's where you hid the bodies."

Lanny furrowed his brows curiously and evoked a look of fear. "How did you know?"

"I don't know."

Lanny nodded. "You're linked closer to your grandma than I thought, kid."

David said, "What children? You're not talking about all those unsolved missing children?"

"It's true. There's gotta be at least eighty skeletons down there. Guilty as charged."

"Why?" David almost whispered.

"Because! It never stops—she never stops!"

"Who?" David questioned, looking at everyone.

"Who do you think?" Lanny replied. "My mother. Ethel. You think she's gone, don't you, David? You're the weakest chain among you three. I didn't think she'd actually come back, but she has, and she's even stronger now that she's disembodied. Then again, who wouldn't be after spending 147 years inside a physical vessel?"

"What are you saying?" David asked. "That Ethel Crowley lived until she was 147 years old? That her spirit's come back from the dead?"

"I wish I were you," Lanny said, lowering the gun a little. "Ignorance is bliss. Now, get over there."

He poked David in the back with the barrel of the revolver. Once he got him and Danny into the shadows, he cuffed David to one wall and Danny to another. David looked into Amy's eyes, confused and delirious. She nodded and said, "It's true. Danny was right all along."

Still, he couldn't seem to believe it. But maybe belief wasn't the right word; maybe he just couldn't come to accept it.

Danny crouched in the far corner, unable to stand since the restraint connected him to the floor. Mom tried reaching for him but didn't have enough space. Lanny stood back and stuffed the gun into a pocket. The light silhouetted him, turned him into a black outline in this cold, stinky room. He stood there looking from one Willow to the other, as if debating, deciding.

"If you just let us go—" David started.

But Lanny interrupted. "I'm not letting you go. We've already established that. None of you are going home tonight. Maybe never again. By morning all three of you might be dead. I don't know yet, myself. It depends."

"On what?" Mom cried.

"On what Ethel wants. She and the black goat."

"Of a thousand young..." Danny mumbled.

Lanny turned to Danny, and Danny knew he was smiling approvingly, even in the dark. "Right, Dan. You catch on quick, but that's to be expected."

David shook his head, as if trying to clear water from his ears. "Could you tell me—tell us—everything? Don't we have a right to know before..." David was starting to sound pathetic.

"Yes," Danny blurted. "Tell us, please?"

Not only did he want to know—*religiously*—but knew that if Lanny blabbed on for an hour or so, that'd buy them time. The gun scared him. Lanny scared him more. But what scared him most was what he imagined arriving later on in the night.

"Well," Lanny said, "I don't know how much you know—not even you, Dan, but I'll explain what I know as well as I can. It's quite a tale. Some mornings I wake up thinking it's been a long, drawn-out nightmare."

He pulled up a folding chair, sat in it, and leaned forward, into a narrow shaft of light. "This all started back in the Dark Ages. The first Crowley to even be born. She was a peasant who became a servant and then, eventually, a witch. According to the old texts, this woman was said to have an eye for opening gateways."

"Gateways?" David's doubt persisted.

"Doors. Call it what you want; it's all the same. Doors, windows, gateways, portals, rips in the fabric of time and space. Just another way to say other dimensions. These exist around us at all times. They change all the time, just as our world changes all the time. Their changes affects ours, and ours theirs, and all the others as well. Some are very distant and hard to reach, even from this place. But others—especially the darker realms, are much closer and easier to open. For instance, if you have someone who's open to temptation, he may be *being* tempted, whether indirectly or directly, accidentally or purposefully, by an entity from one of these lower worlds."

"And they're around us? All the time?" Danny asked.

"We share the same space on different frequencies. What's easier? To build and create a hundred planets or to combine one that endlessly overlaps itself? We have souls, don't get me wrong. Life never ends, and in the case of my mother and her connection to Danny, it appears that death sometimes never ends. The problem stems when these planes connect to one another. For whatever reason, we're not supposed to be able to do these things. Not even Ethel knows the reason to that. Only the more advanced spirits have that answer."

Danny said, "What did the first Crowley do that caused all this to happen?"

"Everything. She was able to conjure demons by mixing potions and ingesting them. A natural. Since nobody knows exactly where she came from, theory suggests she may not have been birthed a mortal. Ethel believed she was a demigod. A master witch who came into existence via cosmic powers during celestial events."

"Like Jesus or something?" David patronized.

Lanny scowled at him. "Something. Halgert showed up in a village one day, bubbling around, looking for food, confused, quiet. An alchemist by the name of Kaesinger took her in. Though Kaesinger was quite advanced in alchemy, Halgert taught him things he didn't know and that she had no way of knowing. She concocted serums that you could rub on your body to render yourself invisible. According to one Grimore, there are supposedly hundreds of potions—using nature—that can make the conjurer perform any miraculous feat. Flight. Invisibility. Teleportation. Telekinesis. Pyrokinesis. Cheating death." Lanny looked at Danny.

"She cheated through me, didn't she?" Danny muttered.

"You're very wise. Ethel herself was capable of doing almost all of these tricks—I call them tricks, because that's what they are.

No more than cheap displays. They've been around since the beginning of time, given to us by Nature Herself, but just hard to learn without some natural spiritual intellect. Flying may seem like magic to someone who hasn't done it, but to someone who knows the trick, it becomes mundane. This doesn't just apply to dark arts and tainted souls; there are good spirits who can do these things as well, but chose not to because they know how cosmically unimportant they are. And sometimes there are more than one way to do the same trick.

"But it's this physical realm that stopped Ethel. She thought she'd live in her body forever, but no magic in the world can stop dirt from eventually rotting... at least not forever."

"And Crowley managed to outlive everyone?" David asked.

"Perhaps."

"What's she want with Danny?" Mom asked.

"His vessel, his body. As long as I'm alive and Danny's connected to her, she will never quit. Just as stubborn as we knew her, huh, Sis?"

"Why him? Why not me? Why not some other child?"

"Because Danny's in her blood. Because he's still young. And because he linked her to himself."

"Link?" Danny said. "How did I link her?"

Lanny stared at him, grimacing. "I can't tell you that. And as long as Ethel is around, you're never going to find the answer to that."

Mom said, "Can't she use someone else?"

"Sorry, that's not the way it works."

"What about all those other kids?" David said. "The ones Danny mentioned were in the well out back?"

"A means to an end. They were for sacrifice. Without them, she wouldn't have attained the power to accomplish all this."

David laughed manically. "So, your brilliant potions and elixirs simply rely on children's blood to work, don't they?"

But Lanny wasn't laughing. "A child's blood is the most potent elixir of all. We needed Danny's blood too, you know. All those Sundays you guys came out here for dinner... I drugged Danny so he'd fall asleep on the couch, and while you were distracted, busy, Ethel drew blood from his foot. Just enough to sustain and draw strength. That's why you were always tired, Dan."

"And pale," Mom mentioned.

"That too." Lanny looked at his nephew. "Dan, I'm sorry for everything that's happened to you. Everything I've done, Ethel's done."

"Then why are you doing this?" David shouted.

"Because. Despite those displays of trickery, there is magic in all the worlds here and around us. Demons. Take one glimpse into their eyes and a part of you ceases to exist forever. I haven't been the same since. You won't be, either."

"Won't be?" Mom swallowed hard. "You mean..."

"Yes. You're going to see the black goat tonight."

David snickered. "What black goat? Some kind of miracle?"

Lanny wasn't laughing or smiling. He remained still and eerily stoic. "A gatekeeper of one of the lower realms. A place between our world and some form of hell."

"Hell?" David sounded dubious.

"Hell's not what you might think, but it exists, and it's mighty terrible. I just hope that Ethel lives up to the deal and helps me bypass it, after all I've done for her. And to others."

David raised his voice. "So you're just a pawn, a coward who couldn't say no to his own mother, aren't you?"

Lanny looked coldly at him. "No. I'm just a victim in all this mess, like yourselves."

"That's a crock," David belted out. "Is he right? Is Danny telling the truth when he mentioned the bodies of all those missing children out in the well out back?"

Lanny said nothing.

"You could've stopped Ethel," David spat. "You could've stopped all of this from happening in the first place. She's hundreds of years old and she overpowered you? That's not being a victim; that's loyalty. You're loyal to her, and to your slaving."

Lanny jumped up, as if spring loaded. "No! You have no idea what you're talking about, *David*. You still don't believe. But you will. When you see, you'll believe, and when you believe, you won't be able to see anymore... not anything good. Everywhere you go, there'll be the imprint of *it* in your vision, always in the back of your mind, stalking you, watching you, waiting. You'll always wonder just what surrounds you. Whenever you're anxious, you'll ask yourself if it's just anxiety or if negative souls are present, heckling you. You can go nowhere without being aware of what lurks in your surroundings. These entities aren't human, not the worst ones, and just glancing into their eyes can render a logical man insane."

David shook his head. "You talking about yourself? Logical man insane, huh? More like an insane man from the start who was never logical in the first place because his mother messed with his head."

Lanny got up and aimed the gun at David, who didn't cower or flinch. He stared into the barrel like a warrior and never blinked once. "Shoot me. Shoot me, be done with it, and let Danny and Amy go."

"I'd love to, David, but that's not my job. If I shoot you, I'll upset the black goat and Ethel. They're one in the same now, in death."

Danny sat in the corner, scared but okay, the floor beneath him cold and hard and dirty. A draft was coming in from somewhere, hopefully outside and not some evil dimension. He didn't feel anything inherently negative, anyway. His dad, laud him, seemed a lot more angry than frightened, but his mom, bless her, was bawling, her constant wails paining Danny's tender heart.

"Mom?" he whispered.

She turned and looked at him. "Are you okay, honey?" she asked, her voice weak and exhausted.

"We're gonna get through this, Mom. No matter what, we'll get out of this. Somehow."

She smiled, or tried to, but it was strained and unbelieving. "I love you, Danny. I'll always love you."

"Don't give up. There's gotta be something we can do."

But she looked right through him, her psyche frayed, her resolve gone. Her body shook every now and again when she switched position.

Danny desperately wanted to save his family, but had no idea how. The realness of the situation hadn't really taken hold yet. The gun in Lanny's hand didn't seem completely real, nor did his true intentions. This almost felt like a child's game. The horrifying visions of his grandmother felt more believable than Lanny—Lanny, of all people—holding them hostage with a revolver. And much more frightening. To Danny, his uncle didn't even seem like a threat. And maybe he *was* sorry for his actions. Maybe he hadn't had a choice. Maybe, just maybe, he was a victim, too.

"Lanny," Danny muttered.

"Dan," Lanny replied, looking down at him. His bald head reflected some light, but his face remained hidden in shadow.

"Why are you doing this to us?"

"If I don't, I won't sleep. I won't eat. I won't be able to function. I'd be dead and in a world far worse than this one."

"Now's the time," Danny said, "that you make a choice, don't you think?"

Lanny aimed the gun at him, but it looked like an involuntarily reaction. David immediately shouted, and Amy squealed. Danny never turned away from his uncle, whose black-shrouded face, he was almost certain, evinced pity and resolution.

Things got real—and unreal—soon enough. It all began with the lights flickering, going out, coming on, and repeating this disorderly display for about a full minute. This was followed by the harsh, cold wind that brought with it a reek of something inherently more foul than rotting meat or human feces. It intensified slowly, steadily, growing, building, worsening. Weapons, hanging from pegs on walls, started moving, hitching forward, about to tumble to the ground, which started to vibrate and quake. Mom wept, Dad observed the developing mayhem, but Lanny looked the most afraid. For the first time tonight, the gun in his hand was shaking, shaking like the weapons, like the pull-string light switches, rattling like the old boards propped up against the wall. Danny watched him closely.

All the lights in this substitute dungeon flickered chaotically, with the speed of strobes, and began changing, jumping from hue to hue as whatever supernatural force bore its way through the tunnel of time and space. The stench became so awful, it made David heave. It made Amy cough. It made Danny's stomach roil. Lanny's throat constricted. He was there, wasn't, was, wasn't, was, wasn't, and the air around him took on a strange ethereal shape that didn't make sense. It warped inwardly, bent, refracted light. They could all feel what was coming, even dad now, because he began screaming, his face swiftly reddening. The rumbling turned so violent, one of the walls cracked. The crack grew and widened and spread, wrecking the room. Lanny held aim on Danny, as if Danny were to blame for all this and needed shot, pronto. It all felt painful, dreadful, terrifying, as if it would go on forever.

Then there was darkness. A Stygian blackness darker than coal. And something was with them... something much older than Ethel Crowley and far more menacing than a revolver.

The silence was foreboding, the still in the air interrupted by a powerful force none of them wanted anything to do with. Danny was anxious to see it. They were all about to witness something as old as the earth, that predated man, and possessed arcane knowledge they'd never know. The black goat of a thousand young. Danny was certain.

The light then came from every direction, a foul, repulsive purple-pink illumination from no known source or point. The entire basement was bathed evenly in this phantom glow, granting them the ability to see what had come from the depths of hell, the long stretch of time unknown.

It looked slimy, but not in a physical, wet way. The glistening goo that surrounded its ethereal body seemed to be some kind of lubricant, perhaps a cocoon for suitable access into their particular dimension. There were eyes, at least seven of them, of undefinable colors and odd shapes, spaced randomly about its obscure form. Its alligator-like face bore an expression that was wholly inhuman and profoundly unholy. It had limbs, all of which corresponded to the anatomies of different animals, both warm and cold-blooded. The black goat didn't stand or sit but appeared to float, to defy gravity. And it could see *into* them. It could see their past sins, their innate flaws, and regarded them with pure, unadulterated enmity.

The air thickened, became more difficult to breathe, and noise from henceforth sounded distorted and dreamy. Though light radiated off this entity, it was still one of the darkest things in the room, a phantom Danny couldn't pry his eyes from. Seeing the picture had been bad, but seeing it in the flesh was a thousand times worse, making Danny feel overwhelmingly sick, mad, detached, and not completely lucid.

Dad, mom and Lanny were looking at it, too—Danny realized this without looking at them.

It didn't move; it simply floated, attached or subdued by a silver cord protruding from its behind. Barbs covered this tail-like substance, and standing behind it, controlling it, was Ethel.

She was not the woman Danny had known. She had never been anything but demonic to begin with. All her cheap smiles, fake hugs, and betraying kisses had been for show, for trickery. Means to fool him. She had never loved him, never cared, and he had never been anything but an instrument for her use, just as she was using this demon now. Danny *hated* her. The rage he felt boiling inside would have offset the fear, had the fear not been so keenly paramount. He wanted her to die, to be dead, to cease to exist, and wished these things on both a conscious and subconscious level.

The demon didn't speak first; Ethel did. Her voice was commanding and resonant and grinding, an insult to any human ear. "The time has come! It's been set. I've dreamed about this since I came into the world many incarnations ago. It's never worked in the past, for reasons I'm not about to tell you."

"Why!" mom shrieked. "Why Danny?"

Ethel turned to her daughter. "Oh, a mother's love, huh, my offspring? Love has no value, Amy. It's an unreal emotion that's reserved for weak, mundane souls who think co-existence is the key to life's survival. Couldn't be further from the truth."

"But why?" mom grunted.

"Because, the stars are in their rightful place. So is Danny. Events like these don't happen very often, my child. It takes much work and time and patience to do what I'm going to do."

"Don't you take Danny! You hear me? Take me instead. Take me, not him."

Ethel's smile faded. "You were nothing in all this, child. It was Danny I wanted before you were even conceived. See, he's my key back to life, a living Dark Trinity—me, the Black Zodiac, and the Goat here. Together we will attain the powers of a reverse Godhead."

Amy sobbed. "God... head?"

"Yes, the keeper of life. And death. Of all things. He's got the all-seeing eye, but what you don't know is that he can't see us now. There *are* spells to shun him out of places, I assure you."

David said, "You plan to become the Almighty?"

"I will become God. The plan's already in motion. When I rule, light will turn to dark, good will bow to evil, and I will live forever when I achieve my status in the next universe. It's been my destiny, my spiritual goal, since my first incarnation, many hundreds of years ago. Oh, and this is just the beginning. The beginning of the end for all of you. I will wreck afterlives. I will harvest from you. I will turn your minds into painful, painful states!"

She grimaced. The baby fingers jutting from her gums, wiggled.

"Why, Mom?" Amy cried.

"Why did you become a mother?" Ethel asked.

"What? Because I wanted to have a child, to love, take care of—"

"No. It was in your biological makeup. A need to latch onto your psyche. It was your destiny. This is mine, and there's nothing you can do or say to get out of this, not even if you place your life before his. Not even if you beg and plead. You don't matter."

Amy cried, and David held her hand. The demon emittcd a grunt or groan that Danny felt in his bones. Any louder and he thought his joints would snap. And even though the monster surrounded by the awful pink light was hideous and fearsome, Danny thought it couldn't quite hold a candle to Ethel.

Lanny stepped out of the way. Ethel and The Goat came forward, floating, gliding, making Danny sicker as they drew near. The air around them warped and vibrated. Amy started screaming, her shrill vocals breaking Danny's heart. Somehow, she got out of her restraint and dove onto the ground in front of him.

"Oh my god," David said.

Ethel corrected, "Soon, when you use that expression, you'll be meaning me."

Danny looked down at his mom, who lay in front of him, guarding him with her life. When he looked closer, he saw how she'd managed to get her hand out of the cuff. Her wrist was broken, the bone poking through the skin, a really visceral sight.

She would do this for me? Go this length to protect me?

She cried and screamed but never moved.

"Stop this," David cried. "Anything. We'll give you anything."

"Oh, yes, you will." They advanced, Ethel and her pet demon, coming to claim Danny, and for perhaps the first time in his life, he realized how much his mother loved him. She'd do anything for him, even if that meant putting her life or eternal soul on the line.

"Don't," Danny said. "Please!"

Ethel seemed to suck in his plead. Then she smiled, and the baby fingers grew from her gums. Things moved and writhed in her mountain of hair, but when she became more visible, Danny noticed they weren't bugs at all, but strands of hair moving on their own. He waited to be possessed, to not exist anymore, when he suddenly remembered Lanny standing by the wall with the revolver in his hand.

Danny looked at him and displayed the most pitiable look in his arsenal. "Lanny? Why? What did I—what did we ever do to deserve this?"

The bad plethora of odors worsened as the demon and its master inched forward. Mom cried but lay steadfast in front of her boy. Dad started shouting, although his voice, to Danny's ears, sounded miles away.

"Extend your arm, Danny," Ethel demanded.

He paused. He noticed that she was carrying a crystal in her free hand. The tip looked very sharp. The grimace on her face made him vomit. The regurgitation landed on his mother, who he wrapped an arm around.

"Stop this!" David shouted, jerking at his restraint.

The unholy light was bright and soul-crushing by this time. More features of The Goat became visible, and Danny wished they hadn't. This image felt seared into him like a brand. Ethel held the crystal like a knife and came closer, obviously savoring the moment.

Danny turned back to Lanny, only half-conscious. The world wobbled around him. But Lanny, to Danny's surprise, was aiming the gun—at whom or what, he wasn't sure.

"Extend your arm, boy, or I'll murder your mother here and now!" Ethel commanded.

Amy bawled and shook. Danny offered his unrestrained hand

and waited for the end to come.

His equilibrium spun as stark panic took hold. *Soon, I will be no more...*

But then, there was another sound, a loud *pop!*–one that reminded him of firecrackers exploding during the Fourth of July.

Lanny. He'd fired the gun at the bottom of the stairs, right where the portal had opened up moments ago. Ethel screeched, her mouth shrinking and distending at the same time. The demon's eyes widened, all seven of them. The light dissolved, or retracted, and the air grew less heavy. Ethel and The Goat were sucked backward, into the preternatural vortex, at incredible speed. As soon as their abhorrent forms were out of sight, everything returned back to normal.

They were left in complete darkness and dead silence, with gunpowder smoke permeating the air. Mom had stopped crying. David had stopped shouting. Danny suddenly passed out.

***

It all came back to him awhile later, when his mother woke him up from a deep sleep. Her hand was wrapped in bandages, and David was free from the handcuffs. Lanny was gone; his revolver lay on the ground, the barrel pointed at the wall where he'd fired the shot. Ethel and The Goat were nowhere to be seen, and neither was Lanny.

"Danny? It's all right now," his mom told him.

They wrapped their arms around each other and cried. "I love you, Mom."

"I love you too."

He'd never told her and meant it as much as he did right now. And he vowed to never again blow off her *I love yous* out of embarrassment.

He held her and felt what he thought could only be her soul.

The authorities had come at nine that morning after mom had

run next door to get help. Apparently, they had experienced a period of lost time since being chained by Lanny, whose body they found lying under the steps, torn to bits and looking like hamburger. Forensics took pictures of it, confused, gossiping about what might have happened. Mom and dad did their best to describe the horrible events. The wall that Ethel and The Goat had emerged from was cracked, dotted with a nice round hole from Lanny's revolver. There was no evidence of Ethel or the thing she'd brought with her. The whole ordeal felt like it was over. A bad memory that wouldn't be easily forgotten, but a nagging splinter that would hopefully dissolve over time.

It had to, because time healed all wounds, didn't it?

During the drive home, nobody said so much as a word. The experience was too fresh, and they'd endured too much in too little time. Both David and Amy's hair had turned white in some places. Their eyes were not the same, either. *Neither are mine, I'm sure.*

By noon, they were home, sleeping. Sleeping and drained. It was one of the most relaxing slumbers Danny had ever had. No dreams intruded. And when his mom woke him up sometime around four in the afternoon, he felt liberated.

He lifted his head off the pillow and looked out his bedroom window. The snow had stopped falling; it was mostly melted by now, and the waking nightmare was finally over.

Chapter Nineteen

They ordered out that afternoon. Dimario's Pizza, Danny's favorite.

They ate quietly at the dinner table, devouring the food like a family of vultures. Danny ate five slices before he threw in the towel. David belched and sipped wine from a glass. Mom finished hers and chugged down a beer. Danny asked if he could have some wine—a question he'd received several stern *nos* from asking before—but this time, both of his parents acquiesced.

They let him have two glasses, which he gulped down in a short amount of time. Dad said enough, and Danny went back to his bedroom feeling fine. He fell back to sleep at six, and slept until early the following morning.

He woke at dawn, as the rising sun revealed its round form over the houses of Tinney Lane. Lemon-yellow light filtered into the room, which he gave a cursory scan, just to be sure. No Ethel, no demon. Just an empty bedroom occupied by a shaken teenager who'd been through hell.

Well, pretty close.

His mom told him that he didn't have to go to school today, that he could stay home until next week. It sounded like a dream come true, but he wanted to go. Or rather, he just wanted things to return to normal again. The more familiar, the better.

So he went. He went and learned, tried to move on, haunted only by the lingering residue of what happened. As the day wore on, though, that lingering residue dissolved slowly into virtual oblivion. He looked over at Randy's desk every now and again and ached whenever he didn't see his friend sitting there.

The teacher was especially nice to him for reasons he could not understand, complimenting him, patting his back, and some of the kids who usually dismissed him offered him either a greeting or a nod. He learned about algebra, about biology, and thought back to the topic of photosynthesis days ago, and about what it had to do with Grandma Crowley. She'd been a plant, in a way, feeding off him, sucking him dry, using his energy to flourish like trees did with sunlight and rain.

After school, when he returned home, his parents gave him firm embraces as soon as he walked in the door, and for a moment, he thought something was wrong. But their sunny smiles upset any momentary lapse of fear. His dad had bought a box of his favorite cupcakes—Donies—from the bakery downtown, just blocks from where he went to school. The aroma of pure sugar sweetened the air—quite literally—and he wasted no time in devouring a few.

"Jeez," his mother said. "You don't have to shove them into your mouth like that."

Danny smiled, savoring all the sugary goodness infiltrating his mouth. Mom laughed. Dad stepped out to use the bathroom.

"I was hungry," Danny said. "We haven't gotten these for a long time."

"Oh, hasn't been long, just a couple of weeks. It only seems long because..."

The awkwardness stopped her. She looked away and crossed her arms, rubbing them as if there were a chill in the air. Danny watched her and nodded. "It's okay, Mom, Lanny stopped them. He stopped both of them."

She smiled. "Good news, Danny, I almost forgot to tell you, and it's been on my mind all day. Regina called."

Regina was Randy's mother, an overweight, over-the-hill hag with long, stringy hair and crossed eyes. Knowing that she'd called and had good news, meant only one thing: Randy was showing signs of improvement.

"She said he opened his eyes a little today. That his stats are getting better. Said he actually talked."

"What did he say?"

"Well, she wasn't sure, but thought that he'd asked for you. The doctors, she told me, have faith he's going to pull through.

Isn't that great?"

Danny smiled. "It's awesome. We'll have to visit him sometime soon."

"Yeah, well, it depends on the circumstances, honey. Nothing too soon."

"Oh, okay."

"But, yeah, soon."

They wrapped an arm around each other. She kissed him on the head. "I think he's gonna pull through; he's a tough kid."

"I hope so."

"That's all you can do is hope. Hope and pray. If there's monsters like... out there, then that's gotta mean there's angels out there, too."

His smiled expanded. He agreed with her one-hundred-percent. To have good, you needed evil, and to have evil, you needed good. The two weren't mutually exclusive; they co-existed because they complimented each other.

Danny had faith in Randy. And he couldn't wait until his best friend was up and back to his old self again. He had so much to tell him, so much to share. He missed his old friend and thought suddenly, had it come to that? Old friend? It hadn't been that long he'd fallen, but it felt like a lifetime ago.

The well...

Police, his mom informed him sometime later, had discovered the skeletal remains of eighty-one children hundreds of feet down in that black pit, victims of witchcraft, evil, sorcery. Danny could barely believe it. Eighty-one dead children, most, of whom, he imagined, had been younger than he was at the time of their deaths. One cop even reported they found a skull with no visible signs of teeth.

A baby's skull.

How messed up was that?

The coppery whiffs he'd always caught had, indeed, been the choking stench of blood. Coagulated and rancid, it had mixed over time with rain and mineral deposits. Traces of blood left behind from Ethel's poor, defenseless victims. What was so important about them anyway? Or about the *fruits of innocence?*

Also, Danny couldn't stop thinking about what Lanny had said shortly before his death...

"I couldn't tell you that."

What secret had Lanny kept? What secret, indeed?

Danny also wondered why Lanny had changed his mind in the end. He'd killed so many children in Ethel's name, and yet, concluded to destroy her when he could have all along. Had he done it for Danny? For mom? Or for himself? To somehow free his conscience? Maybe, in the end, he'd chosen a new path, a different one, and decided to stand up to the beast who'd bore him, raised him, and turned him into the monster she always was.

These were simply unanswered questions he knew he'd have to live with. For now, he spent his time looking forward, waiting patiently for Randy to heal, and to hopefully erase the recent memories from his mind once and for all.

Chapter Twenty

A week trudged by. Maybe flew by, it was hard to tell. Time still felt aberrant, warped. He went to school for a week without incident, and actually made new friends. He even met a nice girl in class. Penny. A brunette goddess with black eyes and a thin, curvy figure. She'd transferred from Lancing, and couldn't seem to take her eyes off him since he took his seat.

At recess, she sat with him on a picnic table by the football bleachers.

"So that's when I came here," she said, watching kids chase each other.

"Don't worry, this school isn't too bad. I'm just sorry to hear that your dad passed away."

"Well, everyone's got a sob story about something or somebody. What's yours?"

I got a story, but I can't even believe it.

He laughed and looked down.

"What? Are you laughing at me?"

"I'm not." He smiled. A cool breeze brushed his bangs from his forehead and blew her dark hair all about. She put hers in a ponytail.

He glanced out at the football field, watching his peers run, sneak smokes, roughhouse. A boy in a Bulls shirt threw a football that was caught by one of the tallest fourteen-year-old's Danny had ever seen: Paul Henny. People often joked, *are you ever going to stop growing?*

It reminded Danny suddenly of Ethel Crowley rising off the ground without so much as touching it.

"What is it?" Penny asked. "What's wrong?"

He shook his head. "Nothing."

"Are you sure?" She sounded genuinely concerned.

"Yeah. It's nothing. Are you going trick-or-treating?"

"Yeah, with my little sisters. They're dressing up as mermaids, and I'm dressing up as a prostitute."

He snorted laughter.

She laughed too. "What? I'm telling the truth. Why? Are you going out tonight?"

"I might."

"Cool. Maybe we can go together." She gazed into his eyes, kicked her feet about, and smiled. Slowly, she moved toward him, inching closer, closer, lips gently puckering, eyes blinking, smelling of peppermint gum. Here she came, his first kiss, hers too, maybe, two teenagers on a heated collision course. Everything faded into the background: the wind, the shouting kids, the shriek of the bell signaling the end of recess. Then, something unpleasant happened.

Ethel says when!

Like a brick wall, everything came crashing down inside. The normalcy he'd recouped; Penny, his first crush; his hopeful thoughts of Randy. *Halloween is tonight. That means fourteen days is up, today. So, had Lanny stopped her? Is she really, truly, gone?*

"What's wrong? What's the matter?" Penny said.

But he was running in the opposite direction, away from her, away from school, away from everything he wanted back and had almost gotten. He was running back into the darkness, into enemy territory. Only one thought occupied his mind:

"I can't tell you that," Lanny had said.

I gotta know what he said. But how?

Randy. He'd found a lot of stuff on the library's computer, so he might know. Either him or Shawna, Mom's friend.

No, Danny, he told himself. *It's over. Gone. It's time to wake up now. Ethel's dead, Lanny's dead; they're never coming back. Stop torturing yourself. Let it go and move the heck on.*

He wanted to, sorely, but the sour feeling in the pit of his stomach said otherwise.

If I only have hours left...

He needed support. While there was probably no better support in the world than his mom and his dad, he didn't want either of them at the moment. His gut, his psyche, was telling him to hitch a ride to the hospital to see Randy, and that's what he set out to do. This outlandish instinct drove him halfway across the ball field and to the seven-feet-high fence, which he scaled and gouged his hands on. He knew that time was of the essence, so he jumped down on the other side of the ground, where grass transitioned to pavement, and ran away from school and toward the highway, searching for cars. The thought of hitching a ride with a nut who might kill him didn't seem nearly as frightening as the alternative. Picturing a dead 90-pound woman versus a virile 300-pound man with muscles was kind of funny, but she would've mutilated him. Just as she and her demon had mutilated her own son, Lanny Crowley.

The streets were empty; most people were at work, doing their duties, grinding away. Danny was out here running from an unstoppable phantom. He didn't think there was a rock anywhere on the earth that she couldn't find him under. She was evilly omnipresent, and he had no prayer.

Snow began falling hard again, and biting cold rose from the west. Chambers Street looked deserted, the lot mostly empty, covered with dead leaves, a light covering of snow. Not one person in coat came walking down up or down the sidewalk. Ducougery Primary School, which he'd attended just years ago, sat quietly on the corner, every window drawn, quiet. Balls lay motionless in the grass, and all the playground equipment looked unused.

Danny stopped frequently to look and see if he was being watched. He didn't sense someone following him; what he sensed was *nothing,* nobody at all. The town felt like a wasteland, a cold desert. The wind kept blowing, snow kept falling, and he started running again. He darted down side streets, alleyways, through yards, jumped over picket fences, wondering if he'd lost his mind or was having some vivid daydream. He expected Ethel, Lanny, or The Goat to jump out from behind a corner and grab him, but found no sign of them... or of anybody else.

The sky turned from cloudy white to a dark gray. It had been sunny when he and Penny had almost kissed, a potentially great experience now lost in the past. Tears stung his eyes as he darted across King Street. The ground was covered with white drizzle, slippery, slushy. Dead leaves cluttered gutters and sewer drains. Jinken's Grocery, a local in town, had a *Closed* sign taped inside its front window. Friday, they should've been open. There was no reason for them to be closed. The lights were off, the shelves stocked with food. Danny approached, halfway across King Street now, when a loud *Beeeeeeee* made him nearly jump out of his skin. Goosebumps crawled across his flesh as he turned and watched a car screech to a stop before him. He had no time to jump out of the way or really react, other than feel fear launch him. He tensed up the way possums do when they find danger. The blue Seville stopped one, maybe two inches from him, the driver inside laying on her horn.

Inches away from real death, he thought.

The woman could have been old enough to be Ethel, her head barely high enough to see over the curvature of the steering wheel. She looked more confused and surprised than angry and annoyed. Then her face, a wrinkled mask caked with make-up, turned white with realization.

"Are you all right?" she yelled through her window. It was partway open.

Danny nodded, relieved. This was confirmation that the world hadn't disappeared—that he hadn't drifted off the face of the planet.

He went to her window and asked, "Please, Mam, can you take me to Lancing Hospital?"

"Oh my Gosh, are you hurt? Did I hit you? I'm so sorry, young man."

"No, nothing like that. Something happened to a friend of mine. I need to check on him. This is a matter of life and death."

She stared dumbly at him before hitting a switch that unlocked her doors. "Get in."

He did. He got in, and wouldn't you know she was wearing the same repulsive perfume Ethel used to wear.

On the way to the hospital, Danny tried telling himself that Ethel hadn't returned, that she wasn't coming for him sometime today, that he was grossly exaggerating... but he simply couldn't shake the feeling.

If my instincts are right, then it means Lanny had never stopped her in the first place.

He'd tried and failed.

Chapter Twenty-One

Lancing Memorial looked more like a mausoleum than a hospital in Danny's tainted vision. Hospitals had always scared him, because only sick, hurt people came here. A lot of the time, folks checked in and didn't check out. That was a horrible fact of life.

The woman behind the wheel hadn't said much during the drive, just tidbits about her family, immigrants who'd migrated here from Czechoslovakia. It reminded Danny of Ethel and the story Lanny had told him about the Crowley family tree. "We come from a long line of witches and alchemists; I don't think our bloodline was ever truly human."

If this were true, and Ethel was all-powerful—and needed him in order to do whatever she wished—then wasn't it also possible that he had some kind of superhuman powers too?

Even if it's possible, it doesn't matter. It doesn't matter because she's had years to perfect it, along with all those weird rituals. I don't know the first thing about how to fend off evil witches or demons.

The woman pulled up to the main entrance. Danny got out of her car. He looked back to thank her, and noticed her cheery smile. "Thanks... ?"

"Regina."

"Regina?" *That's Randy's mother's name, too!*

"What's your name, young man?"

"Danny."

"Danny? Yeah, I got a grand kid whose name's Danny. He's a good kid. About your age. Loves those Magic the Gathering, Dungeons and Dragons games, he does. He's a smart boy, too. Read all the Harry Potter books. Wants to be a magician when he grows up. Dunno about that." She laughed.

Danny didn't. He accepted this as vital information intended for him and him alone. Their worlds, his and Regina's, had almost collided for a reason. A purpose. She was saying, without knowing, without really thinking: *you have the power to defeat your evils by using your own magic.*

She wants you because you're in her bloodline.

If I can stop her, how do I do it? I need to know what Lanny refused to tell me that night.

He looked up at Lancing Memorial. It loomed over him like a concrete monster, its many dark windows staring right back. Snow fell with the same intensity it had the day Randy had fractured his skull. The wind blew steadily and forcefully from the west. Danny didn't know east from west, not without a compass, but just somehow knew this.

Regina drove off. Danny entered the premises, not without thinking he might not leave. Not alive. The air inside was warm and stuffy, the waiting room filled with people coughing and sneezing. The line to the receptionist booth was long. The place smelled of cleanser—disinfectants custodians used to mask the decaying odors of sickness and death.

He looked at the front desk and the extended line leading up to it. Time was a commodity he didn't have. Patience was a virtue he didn't care about. He needed to find Randy before it was too late.

"Miss!" he said to a nurse who brushed past him. "Can you tell me where—"

"You'll have to wait your turn, young man," she said back. She entered the waiting area, eyes big, bright, and blue. "*Ethel?* Ethel Connely?"

Danny thought, *this is it, Ethel's found me and I'm screwed.* But when the elderly woman in the gaudy clothes stood, wiping vomit from her mouth with a handkerchief, the stark horror settled to something more manageable. He could breathe again. In a fleeting moment, however, his motor functions had nearly crapped out on him.

The nurse asked him, "You wait your turn, now. Are you

alone?"

"Randy Wayde?"

"Are you a relative?"

"Yes! I am." He didn't hesitate.

She blinked her eyes slowly and looked at her chart. Danny didn't like her brusque demeanor, even though she said, "Give me just a few moments. We're really busy today. I'll check and see which room."

Danny's nerves slacked some more. "Thank you. Thank you."

"Mm-hmm."

She took her patient away.

Danny waited. He didn't have to wait long, fortunately, as the nurse returned within just a few minutes. She had a slightly nicer demeanor this time, backed with a smile. "Randy Wayde is in room 404."

That was all Danny needed to know. He rushed by her, got onto the elevator, and rode it up to the fourth floor. He found Randy's room with no problem whatsoever. It was on the east side, past the vending machines and a small waiting area.

Randy lay in bed, all alone in an almost-empty room. Snow fell diagonally from left to right through a large window which granted a panoramic view of the valley below. From here, cars looked like toys, the sky stretched for miles, roads snaked and meandered, and hills undulated all around.

Upon looking at him, Danny felt a queasy knot wrench his stomach. The bandage that encircled Randy's head was splotched with blood. It wound around his cranium like a keffiyeh. His right eye was swollen shut, the bruises still fresh. It took a lot out of Danny to see his friend in such a wretched state.

"Oh God, Randy," Danny said, sitting in a orange contour chair. He couldn't turn away from him, and could barely look at him, either.

His monitor beeped steadily, the breathing machine rising and falling and keeping Randy Wayde alive. Tears burned Danny's eyes as he sat there, jaw quivering on a slacked hinge. "Randy. I—"

Randy slowly, lazily, opened an eye. Danny hadn't expected it, and it steeled him, jump-started his adrenaline. Then Randy spoke, gingerly and calmly, but direly as well.

"Danny..." Randy turned his hand over. Danny held it. His grip was weak, skin soft and cool.

"I'm so sorry, Randy, can you ever forgive me?"

Randy's eye widened so gradually, Danny didn't think it was ever going to stop. "It's not me you've got to forgive."

"What do you mean?" Danny thought that maybe Randy was out of it, confused, not quite here. But then his voice took on a more serious tone. "She's not done with you yet. Today's the day. I saw it when I was lost in the dark place, after my fall. I watched you escape her. But you didn't escape her. All she was doing that night... down in the basement... was mark you."

"Mark me?"

"To seal the deal in blood. It makes things easier for her."

"So she's not gone yet?"

Randy shook his head. "No. She's coming. But I know how to stop her. I know the secret to stopping your grandmother."

Danny listened carefully. "How?"

"You remember the gun we shot?"

"Yeah? What does that have to do with this?"

"'Member how I said the gunpowder residue blows up the gun if you don't clean it out?"

"Yeah."

"Your resentment for her, your grandmother, has kept her alive all along. Your inability to forgive her has created a spiritual residue that grants her dominion over you and over death itself. You've been keeping her alive because of the trauma she's inflicted on you over the years. This was her plan all along. You have the power to untie this bind, except your subconscious doesn't know this. She does."

"I'm unwittingly doing all this myself, you're saying?"

Randy nodded. "All that hate you have for her, all that resentment, all that anger, all that childhood trauma, all the fear, every negative emotion you feel for her gives her power, and gives you less. She pre-built it into your mind to trick you. To fool you. This has been your doing, resulting from her careful manipulation, since the beginning."

"All I have to do is forgive her? Forget all this?"

Randy nodded again. "To stop the most powerful evil, you need to take its power away. There's no other way to do it than to denounce it, ignore it, turn your back on it. But that's not all. The resentment has to go. That anger is like spiritual residue poisoning you. You can't just let go, you have to carry no ill-will feelings. You have to love your enemy. That's the weapon that hurts it most of all."

"I don't know if I can do that, Randy."

"If you can't, you'll be dead by tonight."

Danny mulled over this. That's the secret Lanny had been keeping all along. That's the information Ethel had never wanted leaked. He'd always had the power to do this, and just didn't know because he'd been looking at this from the wrong viewpoint, from rancorous, hate-filled goggles.

But once you drink your own poison, it's not so easy to ralph it back up.

Danny didn't want to forgive her after everything she'd done, and, quite frankly, he didn't know how. How could you forgive someone who'd corrupted your childhood, let alone slaughter all those poor, innocent children? How do you reverse a thought process that you've had ingrained into you by someone else? It was like trying to quit being *natural*, cold-turkey, without a manual on how to accomplish it.

"Help me, Randy, help me." Danny gripped his hand. "I don't know how to stop her."

Randy gave him a smile that eased some of his nerves. "Stop

trying, stop fighting. Don't become something new, just be. The harder you look for an answer, the farther away it always gets from you."

These words were like an epiphany to Danny; they put a new perspective in his heart. The change he didn't think he could make was replaced by an inner light and warmth and comfort he'd never felt before. It was as if an angel had entered his body and given him new life. Doubts fluttered away. His mentality changed, strengthened, and righted. His heart didn't steel, didn't fret; it dropped cumbersome chains he didn't know had existed.

Randy lay there and smiled... smiled... smiled... until he looked past Danny and gasped, his one eye widening and his swollen eye bobbing. The gasp he released through his mouth sounded like a last breath. He wasn't dead or dying, but had locked onto a horrendous sight. Over Danny's shoulder.

Ethel.

It's got to be.

He could feel her presence. And when he turned, he saw the witch standing in the doorway, vile as ever, her face not much different than a dry mummy's in a horror film. Large centipedes, as well as roaches, crawled across the whole of her body, feasting on her flaking, cracked skin. She wasn't smiling, but bore an expression of grim depravity. The clothes that hung from her body looked as ancient as she did, tattered garnets designed by Satan. A brown, rotted monster whom Danny finally knew how to beat.

He didn't turn away or cower or flinch; he stood his ground. She looked unimpressed and stared back, her eye sockets empty, her mouth a jungle of broken teeth.

"So," she said, "you got to him before I did."

Danny thought she meant *him*, but she was looking down at Randy. That's when it hit him. She knew he'd blab the secret, and she couldn't have that, could she?

"You're not going to hurt him," Danny shot back, guarding his friend.

"I can do what I want. I will hurt him, in time. I only wanted to end him. I was coming for you tonight, but now that you're here, I might as well claim your body now, cast your soul into the barrens."

"You're not going to do this, Ethel." When Danny pronounced her name, Ethel took a step back. It wasn't far, hardly one whole step, but she receded a little. There was, however, no change in her expression. She bulked up.

"You think two moments worth of realization is going to outdo my lifetime worth of rituals, of preparing you for this?"

"No, but I ain't going down without a fight."

Randy grabbed his arm. Danny looked down at him. "Remember, mercy."

"Mercy?" Ethel laughed. Not one second later, Randy's monitor began beeping rapidly as his heart-rate skyrocketed. Randy grabbed his chest and tensed up, gasping for air.

"Oh no," Danny cried. "Somebody help!"

Randy writhed and thrashed, his legs pushing the blanket to the floor. Quickly, nurses came to the door, but stopped before entering. They could see her now, too. Danny was in shock.

"Yes, Grandson, I've become strong enough for all to see. Soon, they won't see this revolting form. When I look in the mirror, I'll see what I'm staring at right now."

The nurses paused, mortified by this evil entity. They backed away in long, slow steps. Danny heard the monitor beep louder, faster, and Randy's dispiriting gasping intensified. He knew those nurses were his only hope, so he needed to get Ethel out of the doorway and into the hall. That's what he did.

Danny darted forward, feeling fast, feeling alert, rushing Ethel and breathing in her foul, nasty odor. His motive was to tackle her, but he caught nothing but air and tumbled to the floor, almost taking down a nurse instead. She righted. Danny searched. Ethel had vanished from the spot she'd been standing in. The reek of decay was gone. The nurses ran in to save Randy. In no time, he stopping gasping and the frantic beeping slowed considerably.

"Where are you?" Danny knew she wasn't gone. She was playing a game.

"Make you a deal," she said.

He whirled around. There she was, floating by the desk, where receptionists had crouched in fear. "What deal?"

"I'll heal your friend here, now, if you come with me. All you have to do is submit, and his wound will heal. There'll be no complications down the line. He'll be as good as new."

"And if I don't?"

"You'll both rot in black!"

Some of the bugs crawled out of her and fell onto the linoleum floor, where they writhed in swarms.

Danny hated her, what she had become, but that was inaccurate, because she'd always been this dark in secret. That was *her* secret, though, wasn't it? Lies. Nothing but lies.

"Don't resent," Randy had said.

Danny altered the expression on his face, from tough to gentle. "Why did you have to do this to me? To us? To your own children, my mother, my uncle? We loved you, Grandma."

This declaration scared her, visibly scared her. Her face quivered and her floating form dropped an inch or two. The tips of her toes bent. Somebody in another room up ahead starting screaming frantically at the sight of her.

"Love?" she spat. "What's love got to do with anything? Love is nothing compared to fear and hate."

Danny said, "Love saves lives. Love gives hope. Fear consumes. Hate destroys." He took a step forward, and she landed on her feet. Her heels crushed the pile of bugs on the floor. She stumbled backward, almost falling. In room 418, a woman came running out, the fluttering, untied nightgown revealing some of her birthday suit. Ethel grabbed hold of her by the neck before she could get away.

"Your life for hers?" Ethel asked Danny.

Tears filled the woman's eyes as she went on screaming and trying to get away.

"Don't hurt her," Danny said.

"I'll ask you one last time. Your life or hers?"

Danny cocked his head to the side. "Why did you do all this to us, Grandma? All I ever did was love you."

Without hesitation, Ethel snapped the woman's neck. Her lifeless body crumpled to the floor, her eyes glassy and her mouth a giant O. Danny felt sick to his stomach.

"So," Ethel said, "I can see the frustration in your eyes, the confusion. You still hate me, don't you, Grandson?"

Do I tell the truth? Can I lie?

He followed the advice Randy had given him, and most importantly, his introspective heart. "I did for a while, when all of this begin. But now I realize that all the resentment was for nothing, because you are still my grandmother, a warped and confused soul who needs love, not hate."

Ethel's skin flaked off her withering body. Her eye sockets widened and three teeth fell out of her mouth. Her arms seemed to thin, shrink. She levitated, but as she did, her deteriorating form hovered backward in a pathetic attempt at retreat, toward a panel of windows overlooking downtown Lancing.

"You liar!" she shrieked.

Danny walked forward, and she floated backward.

"No, the only lies are what you tell. All this magic, witchery—they're all lies. They're tricks, nothing more. Those children you had Lanny kill—that's real magic. They were the truth. That's why, because, without them, you wouldn't have gotten where you are."

"Shut up!" She was dangerously close to the rank of windows.

Danny kept advancing, gaining confidence, losing qualm. "I don't believe you're evil, Grandma, just twisted."

"Stop this right now."

"But you need to hear it."

She raised a hand and extended her fingers. Pink light shot out of the tips and struck him in the sternum. Danny immediately stumbled and felt several-thousand volts of electricity surge through him. The pain was jagged, the shock eye-opening. All he could think of, though, was stopping her through helping her. "Grandma, please, this hurts. Why are you doing this to me?" he said gingerly.

The electricity dissipated, and suddenly, she looked like a sad puppy after it's been hurt and comes crawling toward its owner. She looked almost pitiable, standing again and no longer floating, her back pressed up against a window hundreds of feet up from the street below.

"Grandma, I need you. Mom needs you. Lanny needs you."

"Lanny's dead," she shrilled. "I killed him. The Goat killed him."

"The Goat isn't real, and you didn't kill him; you just made a mistake, that's all. Everyone can come back from mistakes. All you gotta do is forgive yourself."

"No. No!"

Danny was now just feet away and coming forward, crowding her against the panel of windows. She thinned, her skin shrinking against her skeletal form. All her teeth fell out and dissolved in thin air. She was transparent, a spirit stuck between the physical and spiritual realm, real and unreal, living and dead.

Danny could feel people behind him, leering, watching, scared, stunned. He walked up to Ethel Crowley and said, "I do not hate you anymore. Everything you ever did to me, to Lanny, to mom, it's all in the past. It's forgotten because it doesn't matter anymore. There is no evil in you or anybody. It's all just a lack of love for yourself."

"Please!" she croaked.

Danny took her by the hand, or tried to, but there was nothing tangible to grasp. She'd shrank to almost nothing. He smiled at her for the last time, opened his hand as if he were letting go of something, and said, "No ill-will feelings, Grandma Crowley. It's okay. I finally forgive you."

That's when the whole panel of windows shattered, glass trickling, Ethel falling, meanwhile turning more and more transparent as she plummeted toward the street. Before she impacted, she disappeared, and nothing, not even the bugs, remained.

Chapter Twenty-Two

Danny found himself bawling so strenuously, he didn't think he'd ever stop. Everything he'd said, every emotion he'd conveyed, came from the bottom of his heart. Letting go of great evil was liberating, but letting go of evil you knew, personally, was divine. Letting go of your own sins was hardest of all, and Danny assumed that that's what he'd really done in the end.

Randy made it out of the hospital three weeks later with no lingering problems. Soon enough, he and Danny were playing again, having sleepovers, and enjoying the fruits of innocence again. The ghost of Ethel Crowley eventually dissolved into what felt like a vague, distant nightmare.

School became easier for him as well. No one really bullied him from that point on, because those who tried received a joke or smile from the boy who'd stopped a powerful witch. No, he knew the universal truth now: forgive everyone, everything, including yourself, because if you don't, it'll leave a destructive residue behind, poisoning you for the remainder of your life.

Chapter Twenty-Three

Heather Marchel lay in bed at 3 a.m., her eyes flitting to every shadow, her ears perking at every noise. The terror had begun the night before, when a hideous man with no eyes and centipedes crawling out of his mouth was standing at the foot of her bed.

After all she and her family had endured, this was one concern too many.

Sara Marchel, her sister, had disappeared six months ago in Ducougery, while on her way to a friend's house. For the longest time, authorities hadn't turned up anything, no whereabouts, no leads, no nothing.

That was until October, when RLNO7 News presented a gruesome story about the sudden discovery of eighty-some skeletal remains discarded at the bottom of a well. Authorities reported that none of them were older than the age of twelve, and some were so young they hadn't even formed teeth yet. Apparently the victims of some sort of occult practice. Though forensics had yet to identify them all, Heather believed one of the found skeletons was that of her sister, Sara.

She lay there wanting to sleep, needing to forget and drift into a peaceful world where her sister was still okay and monsters weren't haunting her.

She didn't get her wish.

The door creaked open little by little, and a bald-headed man came walking in, his eyes gone and his mouth twisted open. In his hand he held a strange crystal that glowed an eerie pink light. He said, "I'm coming for you, Heather. Me and the Black Goat of a Thousand Young. I've got no choice in the matter anymore. You won't forgive me, so this is my penitence. And it's all my mother's fault."

Before you go...

Please **rate** and **review** this novel! Share if you like, and if you don't, I thank you for reading it anyway. I'm always trying to improve as a writer, and my readers' input is **highly** appreciated!

Troy McCombs has been writing since the age of nine, when his third-grade teacher made her students write a short story for class credit. He fell in love with the craft then and has not stopped for the past thirty-one years. His genre of choice is horror, but he also likes to write dramas and coming-of-age stories, as well as screenplays. Troy suffers from a chronic social anxiety disorder, a vice he has been struggling with all his life. He lives with his mother and four-legged friend, Mya, in West Virginia.